"Dogs? You want me to walk dogs? That's not work."

"Here it is. Getting them moving is part of the recuperation process."

She looked dubious.

"Just like people who've had surgery." Zeke stood, placing the first-aid kit on a lower shelf, then made himself not smile when he turned around. "What were you expecting to do on the first day? Surgery? Deliver a calf? Or something simple like drawing blood?"

Olivia didn't look amused.

Puzzled, Zeke drew his eyebrows together. "Lighten up. We get enough serious stuff to worry about here. And the dogs and cats in post-op are confused and miss their owners. It's important enough."

Olivia's expression softened. "Of course. I wasn't thinking." Again she twisted her blond hair around one finger.

Morning light pooled through the window and he had an immediate desire to reach out and see if Olivia's hair was as soft as it looked.

Books by Bonnie K. Winn

Love Inspired

*A Family All Her Own
*Family Ties
*Promise of Grace
*Protected Hearts
*Child of Mine
*To Love Again
*Lone Star Blessings
*Return to Rosewood
*Jingle Bell Blessings
*Family by Design
*Forever a Family

*Rosewood, Texas

BONNIE K. WINN

is a hopeless romantic who has written incessantly since the third grade. So it seems only natural that she turned to romance writing. A seasoned author of historical and contemporary romance, Bonnie has won numerous awards for her bestselling books. *Affaire de Coeur* chose her as one of the Top Ten Romance Writers in America.

Bonnie loves writing contemporary romance because she can set her stories in the modern cities close to her heart and explore the endlessly fascinating strengths of today's women.

Living in the foothills of the Rockies gives her plenty of inspiration and a touch of whimsy, as well. She shares her life with her husband, son and a spunky Norwich terrier who lends his characteristics to many pets in her stories. Bonnie's keeping mum about anyone else's characteristics she may have borrowed.

Forever a Family
Bonnie K. Winn

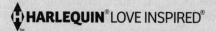

HARLEQUIN® LOVE INSPIRED®

Recycling programs
for this product may
not exist in your area.

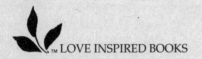

™ LOVE INSPIRED BOOKS

ISBN-13: 978-0-373-87899-4

FOREVER A FAMILY

www.Harlequin.com

Printed in U.S.A.

Be strong and let your heart take courage,
all ye who hope in the Lord.
—*Psalms* 31:24

Dedicated to my agent, Danielle Egan Miller, and my editor, Melissa Endlich. You are deeply appreciated.

Acknowledgment

To Dana D. Clark, DVM.
Thank you for your extraordinary dedication and compassion. I am very grateful that you have cared for our pets with such devotion and personal attention, adding years to their lives they would otherwise not have had. Your incredible care for Doolittle will always remain in our hearts.

Chapter One

Head down, Olivia Gray rushed toward the principal's office, scarcely able to believe her twelve-year-old son, Joey, was in trouble again. Ever since his father had died, Joey had been in scrape after scrape, getting poor grades, ditching classes, talking back to his teachers and getting in fights. She hadn't a clue what to do about him. If she couldn't handle him in Rosewood, what would have happened if they had stayed in Austin?

She flinched at the memory of Ted's murder a year earlier. His death still seemed surreal, a gaping wound where her heart once had resided. A mugging gone wrong. Their lives had been scattered farther than any wind could blow. And her happy, carefree son, who had adored his father, was now almost unmanageable.

"Watch out!"

Vaguely, Olivia heard a man's voice and looked up just in time to see that she was about to crash into him. Stepping to her right to avoid the collision, she plowed straight into him when he maneuvered to his left.

The man's hands were loaded with boxes, and as they each jerked to the other side, her arm whooshed the lid off the top box. She reached out to right the carton, only to collide with him again, tipping the box instead. He knelt, trying to level it. Again trying to help, she grasped one side of the box, offsetting his motion and tipping the entire carton on its side.

Tiny baby chicks tumbled out, running in every direction.

At first unable to believe what she was seeing, Olivia gaped at the fleeing balls of fluff.

"Quick! We have to catch them." The man held out the box lid. "Put the chicks in here when you catch them and then back in the box."

Olivia blinked.

With large hands, he scooped up the nearest chicks, depositing them as he went along.

She hesitated another moment.

"Hurry!"

Realizing the chicks were quickly escaping, Olivia ditched her purse on the floor, clutched the lid and started pursuing the escapees.

She headed toward a small group huddled beneath a bench against the wall. Corralling the chirping chicks was like trying to catch newly blown dandelions.

Plucking them up one at a time, Olivia glanced over her shoulder, dismayed to see what looked like dozens of them still dispersing through the entryway.

She wished the kids weren't in class. They would be able to catch the little things more quickly. A horrid thought struck and she checked her watch. It wasn't too much longer until the bell rang and the halls filled with dozens of middle-school children intent on getting to their next classes, their lockers, focusing on everything but what was underfoot.

She scrambled up, ran the short distance to the office

and flung open the door. "I need help!" Quickly she explained what had happened.

The secretary, Dorothy, jumped up. She signaled to the two student aides. "Come on."

"Let's try to herd them into the office," Olivia suggested once they were in the hall. "Otherwise, when the bell rings…"

No one needed to hear what that would mean. The kids, nimble and quick, clambered to the floor. Olivia was only a step behind, crawling after several baby birds headed toward the side hall. She closed in on them as they were fleeing to the juncture. Reaching out, she grabbed for two of the closest chicks.

And found she was grabbing the strange man's hands. Startled, she stared up at him. Eyebrows drawn together in surprise framed dark blue eyes. An impression of finely honed features continued to the cleft in his chin and the line of his firm lips. Realizing she was still hanging on to his hands, Olivia jerked hers away as she rushed to get up. The abrupt motion unseated him, flipping the box to one side, spilling newly collected chicks into the hallway of classrooms.

His long legs, clad in blue jeans, recovered quickly, but not before the man shot her a look of exasperated disbelief. "Why don't you want these chicks to make it to the 4-H club?"

Olivia's mouth opened, but nothing sensible came to mind. She spun around, grabbed the closest chicks and dropped two in the box. She looked quickly at her watch, realizing there was hardly any time left before the bell rang.

"Late for something?" the man asked, depositing another large handful of chicks.

He was tall, very tall. So she tilted her head back to

meet his gaze. "The bell's going to ring any second. I'm afraid they're about to become roadkill."

The secretary scurried over. "I'm going to ask the principal to delay the bell and make an announcement for the kids to stay in their classrooms. But some kids will manage to slip out into the hall, so be prepared."

"How are we going to know when we get them all?" Olivia muttered to herself.

"Count them."

Embarrassed at having him spell out the obvious, she focused on herding a small flock toward the office. Feeling the brush of something against her back, she pivoted, almost losing her grip on the cardboard.

"It's feed," the man explained, sprinkling some grains in the lid.

"Is it to…?" Her words trailed off as she stared into his remarkably deep blue eyes.

"Helps keep them in the lid," he explained.

"Oh. Good idea…" Her mouth remained open but nothing else emerged, because she didn't know his name.

Apparently he guessed her thoughts. "Zeke." He paused. "Harrison."

"Gray. Olivia," she responded automatically, a result of being an army brat.

Unexpectedly, he grinned. "But you go by Olivia?"

She felt her cheeks warming, her eyes rolling downward a tad. "Yes."

Zeke knelt down on one knee beside her. "Let's put the chicks you collected into the box. It's easier than trying to balance them on the lid while you're getting more."

Olivia allowed him to take the lid, trying not to notice just how long his legs were or the play of muscles in his arms as he offered a hand.

She could have easily risen by herself, yet she allowed

him to help. Her still-shaky hand tingled beneath his and this time she didn't jerk away. Remembering the chicks were still running amok, she gestured toward them with a nod of her head.

Understanding, Zeke released her hand.

Nearly half an hour later, the last of the chicks were caught and all eighty accounted for.

Dorothy, the harried secretary, barely paused. "I'll tell the principal he can release the kids for their next class." She glanced at her watch as she turned toward the office. "It'll be a short one."

Alone with the man, Olivia's sense of awkwardness returned. "Um, I'm really sorry about all of this."

Zeke looked up, his eyes, unbelievably, darkening even more. "No harm done."

"I hope the chicks agree." She shifted from foot to foot. "Good luck with the 4-H kids."

He grimaced. "I'd almost forgotten I still have that to do."

Startled, Olivia checked the time. "And I *did* forget where I was supposed to be. I'd better—"

"Yeah."

Olivia watched his broad shoulders and long legs as he retreated. A lifetime ago, before she had met Ted, she would have appreciated the image. But that was all behind her now. Something else that had scattered beyond recovery.

Once he was out of sight, she reluctantly turned toward the office, wishing she didn't have to face the school principal, wishing as she had so many times that Ted hadn't died. That they were still a family. That her son still had a father, still thought the world was an adventure instead of a terrifying place filled with awful people and danger.

Running nervous hands down her thighs, she entered

the office. Dorothy motioned toward the principal's office. Through the open door, Olivia saw him, along with Joey and his teacher, Mrs. Tonell. Her stomach sank. Instinctively she knew this was going to be bad. "Sorry to be late," she began, entering the principal's office. "You know about the chicks that got loose in the hall...." Her voice trailed off as she spotted a note of disapproval in the principal's eyes. Like mother, like son?

"We're not here to talk about the chicks Dr. Harrison brought," Principal Norrick replied.

Dr. Harrison?

"Please sit down, Mrs. Gray."

Olivia chose the chair next to Joey's, wishing she could give him a word of support or a hug of encouragement, but all eyes were on her. So she settled both hands in her lap, hiding their nervous shaking beneath her purse. These days her hands often trembled, her stomach remained in a perpetual knot and she never stopped thinking about why it was *her* family that had been destroyed.

Principal Norrick stared from behind his desk, his face set in stern lines. "We've been as patient as possible with Joey, but this time we *cannot* diminish the gravity of what he's done. Mrs. Tonell witnessed him stealing an expensive wireless headset from the computer lab."

The unhappy teacher looked nearly as miserable as Olivia felt. "I hoped it was just a quick impulse, that he'd turn around and put it back."

Olivia hadn't thought her stomach could sink any deeper, yet it did. She stared down at Joey, who sat in the rigid wooden chair next to hers. "Is this true, Joey? Did you steal from the computer lab?"

He shrugged, a halfhearted gesture that was neither acknowledgment nor apology.

Reaching over, she slipped her hand beneath his chin and tipped his face up so she could meet his eyes. "Joey?"

"I guess."

She didn't have it in her to be harsh to her wounded child, so she softened her voice. "Either you stole the headset or you didn't."

"Yeah."

Swallowing against disappointment and sickness, Olivia turned back to the principal, waiting for the judgment to be handed down.

"He had been making progress…" Mrs. Tonell began, but her words died when the principal glared in her direction.

"We discussed this in our last meeting, Mrs. Gray," the principal said. "And Joey is aware that he was given his final warning."

Trembling, Olivia faced him, dreading his next words.

"Suspension and working in the library aren't sufficient solutions to this level of misconduct," the principal continued. "I am afraid that only leaves expulsion."

Olivia gasped, then tried to collect herself. "Surely we can reach a compromise that will keep Joey in school." Leaning forward, she gripped the edge of the desk. "I know how very patient you've been since his father passed away, and it's appreciated far more than I can express. But Joey still hasn't recovered." She attempted a small smile but failed. "Neither of us has. I wouldn't ask for special allowances for myself, but a child…hasn't lived long enough, experienced enough to deal with such a loss. But I believe he'll get there in time if he's given the chance."

Principal Norrick glanced over at the teacher, then at Joey, finally settling his gaze again on Olivia. "It is not the school's policy to ignore such behavior…."

Olivia's throat dried up.

Pausing, the principal turned his attention back to Joey for several moments. "We don't often expel students. I think you know that, Mrs. Gray. And it is not something I *want* to do, but the other children can't be allowed to see Joey getting away with this conduct." His sigh nearly filled the dismal air. "There may be one option we can exercise on a probationary status."

Olivia didn't dare breathe.

"Joey will return the headset and he will be suspended for two weeks. He will still be responsible for collecting and completing all of his schoolwork." The principal stressed each word, keeping his eyes on Joey. "In addition, he will be required to work two hundred hours of community service." He turned back to Olivia. "Dorothy will give you details on where to report."

"Thank you, Principal Norrick. We won't let you down."

He studied Joey, clearly upset that a student of his had come to this point. "I hope not."

"You won't be disappointed," she reiterated, ready to escape the adrenaline roller coaster she had been on since entering the school. When her son didn't speak up, she nudged him. "Joey, thank Mr. Norrick."

"Thanks," he mumbled without an ounce of conviction.

The principal stood, and Olivia shot up from her chair and nudged Joey toward the door.

Back in the main area of the office, she tried to gather her wits.

Dorothy sent her a sympathetic smile. "I'm filling in Joey's community-service assignment." She lowered her voice so it wouldn't carry to Principal Norrick's office. "It should be one he'll take to."

"Thanks, Dorothy." Olivia bit down on her lower lip. "Do you suppose there's enough time left today for Joey to pick up his schoolwork from his teachers?"

"Should be." The secretary reached for a different form, then scribbled the necessary information. "Joey, show this to all your teachers and they'll give you what you need."

Looking particularly displeased, Joey accepted the paper.

"I'll wait by the car while you go around to your teachers," Olivia told him as she stashed his community-service paper in her purse. "No dawdling."

He rolled his eyes. "I'm not five years old."

She met his rebellious gaze, making herself sound stern and in control, despite feeling as if she were steering a rudderless ship. "Then don't act like you are."

Walking slowly out to the parking lot, Olivia blinked back the threat of tears. Her late husband would be so disappointed to see how badly she was handling their son.

"Something wrong?" a familiar voice questioned.

She halted, trying to act and sound near normal. "Zeke!" she greeted him, relieved that she remembered his name. "At least I didn't run smack into you this time."

He held up his empty hands. "The 4-H club now has custody of the chicks. All eighty of them."

"Again, I'm sorry about that."

"Unless I'm mistaken, you didn't aim for me."

She smiled.

"That's better." His grin widened.

As she focused on him, Olivia noticed the white Suburban he stood in front of. *Harrison Veterinary Clinic* was painted across the top half of the cab. Dr. Harrison. Baby chicks. The dots began to connect. "Are you a veterinarian?"

"Guilty. That's why I was bringing the—"

"Chicks," she finished for him. "You work a lot with the 4-H club?"

"Some. I'm the only vet for miles, so I do a little of everything."

Being an army brat, Olivia had never owned a pet. Her father had insisted it wasn't practical, since he never knew when they would be transferred. "Probably not so much chick chasing, though."

He started to grin, then forced his lips into a neutral line but failed to disguise the twinkle in his eyes.

It took a moment but the double entendre hit her like a dozen bricks. Chasing chicks, as in women? She winced. "This obviously isn't my day."

"Actually, it was pretty funny."

She wondered if he meant the ill-worded remark or the scattered baby chickens.

Raising her gaze, Olivia saw that he was focused on her. Swallowing, she fought the flood of attraction and the stunning realization that such feelings still existed within her. Olivia thought they were gone forever when Ted died. Disloyalty and guilt warred with the wash of new emotion.

"Mom!" Annoyance magnified the single word.

And she was appalled to realize she had completely forgotten about her son. She spun toward Joey.

He stared at her with his now-standard impatient-twelve-year-old posturing.

"Nice to have met you, Doctor." Olivia put her hand on Joey's shoulder to center herself as she began walking away.

"Zeke," he corrected.

Even though she was several feet away, she heard his name as distinctly as if he had whispered it in her ear.

Chapter Two

Zeke studied the day's appointments. One jumped out at him. Fluffy, owner Belinda Bates. Only Belinda would name an overly manicured poodle *Fluffy.* But he had to hand it to her: she was consistent. In high school she had fluffed her hair, her personality, her values.

But he'd loved her. From the moment she had asked him to the Sadie Hawkins dance in their sophomore year of high school. It seemed that wherever Belinda walked, a glow followed. Popular, pretty—he was amazed that she wanted to date him. He was the resident bad boy, still hurting from years of being bounced around the foster system. And it took time to transition from that rebellious, angry boy into a man. When Belinda started to date him, he was still in the angry stage.

His foster parents made him attend school, didn't accept any excuses and followed up to make sure he was toeing the line. But not like the other homes he had lived in. The Harrisons treated him as their own. They showed him love he couldn't break and an understanding that finally got through to him.

Belinda, on the other hand, hadn't been burdened with the same feeling of obligation.

Pulling open his desk drawer, Zeke stared at the tiny engagement ring he had bought for her so many years ago when he had finished his undergraduate studies at Texas A&M. After they'd gone together almost four years, Zeke had been certain she would accept his proposal.

But Belinda, who had chosen to attend the University of Texas, had had other ideas. He was too much of a wild card, she had said. Zeke exhaled, knowing he would never forget those words. Couldn't be certain of his *real* background, Belinda had explained. And she couldn't have children with someone who couldn't be vetted. No telling how the children would turn out.

He had been stunned, Zeke remembered. Completely flattened. Why, he'd asked, had she dated him all this time? Her eyes hadn't even changed with her admission. He had never noticed that before—her ability to hide her real feelings. Because he was different, Belinda had replied with a small shrug. She'd liked his edge, the way he flouted rules when he wanted to, defied authority. But really, did he think she would marry him? And had he really believed she hadn't dated other guys the past four years? It shouldn't have mattered. He should have forgotten all about her. But despite the changes he made, the encouragement from his by-then adoptive parents, the words stayed with him. Like a measuring stick.

His birth parents had been teenagers, his father jailed for a string of petty burglaries and vandalism. And Belinda, for all her cold disdain, had a point. Zeke had no idea what his genes would produce. Sure, he had straightened out, but that was his adoptive parents' doing. They'd loved him when he was unlovable and had never given up.

"You've seen the appointments, then," Angie said from the doorway.

He didn't need to ask to know she was referring to Belinda.

"She has to be the most insensitive person on the planet," Angie fumed, knowing Zeke's history. "And why you let her bring her neurotic puffball here—"

"It's not the dog's fault," Zeke replied mildly, even though Belinda's gall was insulting.

"You could tell her to take him to a vet in another town."

Yes, he could. But every time he saw Belinda, it reminded him of how blind he had been. How he never intended to be ambushed like that again.

Olivia navigated her car out of town, the school secretary's note in one hand. Joey stared out the window as though she were chauffeuring him to prison. "You know, this community service will go a lot smoother if you approach it with a good attitude."

"Does Grandpa know I'm missing the whole baseball season?"

"He will soon enough." Olivia struggled to find a tone between scolding and understanding. It was difficult enough handling Ted's death as an adult. Joey was just a boy.

"Grandpa won't like it."

"Unless you've forgotten, you could have missed basketball and football next season, too, if you'd been expelled." She didn't tell him that the administration had allowed him to stay on the team during his bad behavior only because they were sympathetic to Ted's unexpected death.

Not having a ready retort, Joey turned back to stare at the familiar landscape. When Ted was still alive, they would all have been chatting about which of the wildflowers continued to bloom.

Inhaling an acrid scent, Olivia scanned the hillsides for smoke. The severe drought had wildfires popping up in the area, and although Rosewood had been lucky, the possibility added to Olivia's stress.

Joey exhaled loudly.

"You know, you still haven't acknowledged the seriousness of what you did. Stealing."

He shrugged. "Just some dumb headset."

"I don't care if it was a marble. It's not how much the item's worth. It's about what *you're* worth. Stealing isn't honorable. And without honor, where is your worth?" She slid her gaze toward him.

Joey's chin drooped a fraction, but he didn't reply, instead turning again to stare out the window.

The early-morning traffic on the highway consisted mostly of eighteen-wheelers and pickup trucks. She had always been glad that the road wasn't connected to a freeway. It gave Rosewood a feeling of protection unlike what she had known most of her life, moving from fort to fort.

Her father, the Colonel, had decided to retire in the Hill Country soon after Ted had graduated from the University of Texas. Joey was just four then. Ted had been offered a good job in Austin right after graduation, so they'd decided to stay. But seven years later, the company had closed its doors.

The Colonel had still had influential contacts from his army days. One of them had suggested a business that Ted could operate from home. Without the anchor of his job, Austin hadn't had a hold on them any longer. Ted's parents had passed away during his college years and he sorely felt their absence. So when the Colonel suggested they relocate to Rosewood, Ted had been elated, wanting to be close to family.

Olivia had had mixed feelings about the move. She'd

lived in Austin longer than anywhere else in her life. But she couldn't deny that it would be good to be closer to her parents. Even though they'd visited back and forth, it wasn't the same as being close enough for impromptu get-togethers, family dinners and special grandparent time.

Ted had liked his new work, but it had required some traveling. They had been in Rosewood only a couple of months when he'd made that fateful trip to Atlanta. When the police caught the suspect, he'd turned out to be a young man, barely more than a boy, who had panicked during the mugging and shot Ted unintentionally. Intentional or unintentional, the result had been the same. Ted had died alone on a strange street in a strange city.

Olivia blinked away the threat of tears, trying to push the memories away, as well. Although they had only lived in Rosewood about a year and a half, she had grown attached to the quiet, caring community. If Ted had lived, by now he would have met every neighbor, introduced himself to every clerk in every business in town. He'd been outgoing and open, and people didn't remain strangers to him for long.

But after his death, Olivia hadn't been able to continue his natural outreach. She had always been more reserved, accustomed to keeping a low profile in the many towns her father had been stationed in. She had learned early on as an army brat that making friends only made it that much harder when they moved.

Most of her acquaintances and friends were ones Ted had made, always trying to enlarge her circle to give her something she had never had before.

Now, having retreated from everything except her son, her parents and a part-time job as a drugstore inventory clerk, she struggled to maintain a normal life for Joey. Olivia questioned if she had failed Joey by being so reclusive. Maybe he wouldn't have gotten into so much trouble if she had involved herself more in the community, made friends, reached out to everyone.

Olivia glanced again at the directions Dorothy had given her. The place was only about five miles outside of town, so the turnoff should be close. She spotted it and turned onto the two-lane farm road.

Cattle grazed behind split-rail fences, unperturbed by her car passing by them. She hadn't seen another vehicle on the road since she had turned onto it. Maybe these cattle were a laid-back breed since they didn't seem at all bothered by her car. Then again, the only breed she could actually identify was the Texas longhorn. The closest she had ever gotten to wildlife was an occasional mouse.

Slowing, she saw an old-fashioned metal sign, engraved with *HVC,* hanging from a post. Just as the directions had described. Turning, she passed beneath a tall wrought-iron arch.

Looked like a peaceful place for her son to rethink his actions. She looked upward, her automatic response to ask the Lord for help. But He had allowed Ted to needlessly die. Clenching the steering wheel harder, Olivia felt she could no longer turn to Him.

She wheeled their car to the front of the old ranch house. A wide wraparound porch encircled the structure. Tall double doors, which appeared to be perpetually propped open, welcomed them at the top of the broad wooden steps. Olivia led the way, Joey trailing her.

Once inside, she took in the large room off to the left that looked like a man's comfortable den. To the right was a reception area. Arched wooden pocket doors as tall as the high ceilings were slid partway open to the den and fully open to the business side.

Not seeing anyone sitting at the scarred wood desk, Olivia entered the reception area. A scattering of mismatched chairs looked more homey than shabby. She could see that the buttons on the telephone were flashing, perhaps on hold, perhaps going unanswered.

"What kind of dump is this?" Joey asked, staring around at the plain but comfortable room.

Olivia closed her eyes, wishing Joey could just be her Joey again. "Hush. We're not in a big city. You know they don't build places in Rosewood to impress people."

"Angie? I need the file on Mitchell's gelding," an oddly familiar voice called out from a connected room.

The man, absorbed in the chart in his hands, walked into sight.

It couldn't be. Could it?

He looked up, his memorable features quickly forming a smile.

And Olivia couldn't think of a single word to say. HVC. Of course. She should have realized the acronym. Harrison Veterinary Clinic.

"Hello," he greeted them with a warmth that she felt from across the room.

"We…" Her voice warbled. Clearing her throat, Olivia started over. "My son has been assigned to do his community service here."

He lowered the chart, his gaze appraising. "I've been expecting you. Dorothy called this morning. Joey, I'm Zeke Harrison. We didn't actually meet yesterday. And I don't believe I've seen you around before."

In typical fashion, Joey shrugged.

Olivia hurried to fill in the blanks. "We've only lived in Rosewood for about a year and a half."

"And your family doesn't have pets?" he questioned, helping the limping conversation along.

Olivia stared into his azure-blue eyes, instantly remembering how she had practically fallen into his arms. She shook her head. "No, we don't. My husband…" Abruptly she halted.

"Your husband?" Zeke prompted, a flicker of something much like disappointment in his eyes.

"My dad was allergic to dogs and cats," Joey jumped in, answering for her, apparently noticing her difficulty.

"Was?"

She recovered her voice. "My husband passed away."

Zeke's expression eased into one of understanding as he looked again at Joey. "I'm so sorry. That must be tough."

"Yeah."

Her son's solitary word summed it up perfectly.

Zeke laid the chart down on the desk. "So do you like animals, Joey?"

"I guess."

"I'll take that as a yes."

Olivia indicated the empty chairs in the reception room. "Slow time?"

"Large-animal time. I reserve two mornings a week for owners who need to bring in their domestic stock but don't need me to come to their places. Less expensive for them that way."

Thoughtful. Olivia glanced down at her son. "Joey hasn't been around…" She drew her eyebrows together in concern. "Exactly what types of large animals do you treat?"

Zeke looked at her in mild amusement. "Not too many elephants and giraffes in these parts. Mostly cattle and horses, donkeys, pigs, llamas, some sheep and goats."

Flushing, she felt as silly as she had on their first encounter.

"My mom's never lived in the country," Joey explained.

Great. Even her sullen child was taking pity on her.

"Of course. I wasn't thinking. So you treat regular pets, too?"

Zeke raised his eyebrows, his amusement still present. "Depends on your definition of *regular*. Dogs, cats, birds, pygmy hedgehogs, ferrets, lizards, snakes…"

Olivia gasped. "Joey won't have to handle snakes, will he?"

"Mom!"

At that precarious age of twelve, poised between childhood and puberty, Joey was utterly horrified.

Belatedly realizing that, Olivia tried to cover her mistake. "I confess, I'm the one who's scared of snakes. Joey's pretty tough."

Joey rolled his eyes, which told her her recovery attempt had been lame at best.

"It's a nice place you have here," Olivia remarked, hoping to change the subject.

"We like it."

"We?" The instant the question was out, Olivia wished she could snatch it back.

"My tech—Angie—the animals, me."

Olivia tucked away the information that he wasn't married. "That's good."

"Well, Joey. What do you say?" Zeke asked. "Want to start today?"

Joey shrugged. "I guess."

"Sounds good," Olivia agreed, looking relieved. "He's out of school for two weeks on suspension, but the time's counted in community-service hours. The sooner he can start and accumulate his service hours, the less school he misses."

Zeke glanced into her memorable violet eyes, recognizing her anxiety. But anxious or not, pretty or not, he had a practice to run and couldn't ease her mind by overloading his own schedule. "Let's just see how the morning goes."

A quick flash of disappointment crossed her face. Then she smiled, her delicate features aligning to match.

"We appreciate you giving Joey an opportunity to do his community-service work here. I'm sure it'll be good for him to interact with the animals." Olivia squeezed her son's shoulder in encouragement. "Well, I should go and let you get to it. Um, what time should I pick him up?"

"How about Joey calls you when he's ready to leave?"

"Sure." She bit down on her lip. "I'll be at work some of the day. I'm an inventory clerk. It's just a small part-time job at the pharmacy, about ten hours a week. But I'll have my cell phone with me. Do you need any emergency contact numbers or—"

"The school gave them to me."

"Oh, of course." For a moment Olivia looked uncertain. "See you later, then."

She turned and he let his gaze stray over her as she left. Being a widowed mother, Olivia probably wouldn't be interested in casual dating, which was all he allowed himself. Belinda had about cured him of any wish for a more serious relationship. Then his previous relationship with Penny had convinced him he wasn't capable of making good decisions when it came to women. Not that Olivia seemed anything like Belinda. At least on the surface.

Joey wandered over to the large aquarium and thumped on the glass, recapturing his attention.

"No tapping on the glass."

The boy furrowed his brow, looking puzzled. "How come?"

"They don't like it."

"Oh."

Could the kid really not know that? "Have you ever had *any* pets?"

Joey's expression remained sullen. "Just a turtle. He mostly sits in his box and eats. My mom didn't ever have any real pets and my dad…"

Zeke didn't make him discuss the painful subject. "It would be like having a tree fall on your garage for the fish when you hit the tank. Pretty jarring."

Joey looked again at the tank with an instant spark of understanding but didn't reply.

"Is your mom allergic to cats and dogs?" Zeke questioned casually.

"No."

"Just doesn't want a pet?"

"Grandpa was in the army, so they couldn't take a pet when he got transferred, so she never had any."

"Your grandfather must have been in the army a long time."

"Forever, until he retired here."

A new picture was emerging. So the violet-eyed beauty was an army brat. He would never have guessed it. But then, his insight into women hovered between zero and none.

His tech, Angie, rushed through the open door, her dark brown hair messy from the breeze. Despite being four months pregnant, the spring in her step hadn't diminished. "Morning!"

"You sound extra chipper today."

She laughed and patted her stomach. "Probably because there's extra me." She turned toward the boy. "I'm guessing you're Joey. I'm Angie."

"Hey."

The unenthusiastic greeting didn't faze her. Angie's glass wasn't just half-full; it was always overflowing.

"Welcome. Later I'll show you where we stash the snacks and soda."

Joey still didn't show any interest. Swallowing, Zeke remembered how he had felt at that age. It was a tough place to travel even in his thoughts.

Exhausted, Olivia closed the front door and tossed her purse on the small table close by. Pressing fingers to her temples, she wandered first to the window, then over to the bookcase. She picked up a picture of her late husband. "Oh, Ted. It isn't getting any easier." Holding the picture close, she remembered how he had been there one day, gone the next. "Joey's gotten into even more trouble. A lot worse than talking back to his teachers, and the fights."

Olivia stared into Ted's steady brown eyes. Joey looked so much like him, down to what had once been a wide, frequent smile.

The empty house echoed in the silence.

"Now Joey's actually stolen. A headset, of all things." Shrugging, she traced Ted's smile. "And he acts like it's nothing."

The doorbell rang, startling her. Fumbling, she replaced Ted's picture. She pulled open the door and was surprised to see Kate… She couldn't place her last name. "Hi." Trying to compose herself, Olivia opened the door wider. "Please, come in."

"I hope I haven't come at a bad time," Kate replied, surreptitiously looking into the living room.

Olivia shook her head. "It's…it's fine."

"You don't have company?"

Olivia flushed, realizing Kate must have seen her talking to Ted's photo while standing in front of the picture window. "No one alive."

Since Kate's husband, Tucker Grey, was Rosewood's

sheriff, she had been one of the first to learn about Ted's death. She had made efforts to reach out, but Olivia's parents had circled the wagons. And Kate had tactfully withdrawn. Until today.

Olivia pulled herself together. "Don't mind me. One of those days. Please, sit down. Can I offer you some iced tea?"

"You read my mind. Need any help?"

More than she could voice. "No, it's all made. Do you take yours sweet?"

"Just plain. I save my calories for cookies and candy." Barely having landed on a chair, Kate stood up. Trailing Olivia, her sandals clicked on the wooden floor. "When I'm antsy, I eat extra goodies, so it's good I like my tea without sugar."

Olivia reached into the cabinet for glasses.

"Did you say the tea's already made?" Kate asked, pausing at the refrigerator door.

"The pitcher's in the middle on the right."

"Lemons in the fruit drawer?"

Amused, Olivia hid her smile. If this was Kate not helping, she could only imagine when she pitched in wholeheartedly. "So is something making you antsy?"

"Afraid so. Do you want to sit at the table?" Kate gestured to the round table. "Kitchens always seem friendlier to me."

"Cozy." The word popped out. Funny—she hadn't thought anything had been cozy for so long. She reached into a cabinet and pulled out a box of coconut macaroons.

After they'd settled at the table, it didn't take long to pour the tea, squeeze a few slices of lemon.

"You're probably wondering why I showed up without calling," Kate began. "But I'm desperate."

Olivia raised her eyebrows.

Kate immediately scrunched hers together. "I don't mean for company. That came out all wrong. I get this way when I'm frazzled. Did I ever tell you how I met Tucker?"

Olivia shook her head.

"I won't go into detail, but I was frazzled to the max. Still amazes me that he ever proposed." Kate's green eyes softened. "Sorry, I also go in about a hundred different directions when I feel like this."

"Like what?" Olivia prompted gently.

"Sorry, it's about a project I'm working on. Or not working on, I should say. I've been commissioned to do a new painting."

"You're an artist?"

"You didn't know?" Kate's surprise glided into a smile. "I trained first as an artist, then in restoration. I primarily worked on museum pieces. Now they give me referrals for different types of work. That's how this family found me." Kate stopped abruptly. "I don't know why I assumed you would know I'm an artist. We haven't really talked a lot. I know—" her chipper voice changed notes "—that it hasn't been easy for you." She met Olivia's eyes. "I don't know what I would do if I ever lost Tucker." Amazingly, she wiped away a tear.

And Olivia reached out. "It's all right."

"No, it's not. But I suppose you can't say that, that it's awful, I mean. You always have to be brave for your son."

"You know Joey?"

Kate's eyes darkened and her expression dimmed. "Not really. Not firsthand."

The school theft. Of course the sheriff had been informed. Olivia felt the heat that suddenly colored her face.

"Please don't be embarrassed. If Alyssa lost her dad… She already lost her first mother. Her world would just about end."

Confused, Olivia tried to remember what she could about Kate's family and came up blank. "You're not Alyssa's mother?"

"Her mother died when she was ten. I met Tucker about two years later. Since then, I've been her mom."

Olivia instinctively sensed that theirs was a true mother/daughter relationship. "That's lovely. I don't think I've ever really seen that happen before. Becoming a child's real parent after a death, I mean."

"I was…I *am* very fortunate. It's hard to imagine that anyone else can take on that role once you've lost your spouse." Absently, Kate circled the top of her tea glass with one finger. "That's how Tucker felt. It's how I imagine anyone would feel when they really love the person they've lost."

Olivia's throat tightened.

"I'm sorry. I've made you think even more about your late husband." Kate's sunny exterior now wilted in remorse.

"No. I was talking to his picture when you arrived." Olivia again imagined how foolish she must have looked, yet she sensed Kate wouldn't laugh, wouldn't judge. "So he was already on my mind."

Kate reached out a friendly hand. "Is it loneliness or something else?"

Olivia sighed. "Joey. How I'm going to handle him with Ted gone. I never could have imagined him stealing. I understood when he cut classes because he couldn't face people, but this… It's not the way he was raised."

"Of course it wasn't. But how do we teach our children the way to act once they lose a parent?"

Olivia looked down. "Tucker's job—surely that has moments of fear. Was Alyssa taught to know that?"

"He's her hero. She's old enough to know his job can be

dangerous, but it's not something we dwell on." Concern filled Kate's eyes. "You didn't do anything wrong, Olivia. Tucker's told me about kids who haven't handled the loss as well as Joey has. You have to be overwhelmed, suddenly becoming a single parent after years of being able to turn to your husband for support."

Throat still tight, Olivia agreed. "I feel like I'm disappointing Ted, that he'd be horrified at how I've handled things."

"I didn't know Ted," Kate replied honestly. "But as sure as I'm sitting here, I know he would understand. Men are usually more crippled by losing their wives."

Olivia pulled herself out of her self-pity. "It's weird. Before you came, I was just thinking that maybe if I'd reached out, made more friends, that Joey wouldn't have gotten into trouble."

"You can't know one way or the other. But I'd recommend getting him involved with the youth group at the Community Church. The activities—"

"I don't mean to be rude, but that's not an option."

Kate paused, then sighed. "Tucker felt the same way about his faith."

"Besides, Joey has community-service work that takes all his time. He's volunteering at Harrison Veterinary."

"At Zeke's?" Enthusiasm bounced back into Kate's voice. "That's great!"

"You know him?"

"Of course. He delivered my puppies." She laughed. "Well, my dog's puppies, I should say. Nice, nice man. Never could figure out how he's managed to stay single."

Olivia tried to think of a sensible reply. Not able to come up with one, she sipped her tea instead.

Kate checked her watch. "I didn't mean to stay so long. I came to ask a favor."

Olivia couldn't imagine what it could be. "Oh?"

"It's about your dad."

"Really?"

"You sound surprised."

"That's because I am," Olivia admitted. Her father had never been one to mingle into what he called "town life." So accustomed to military forts, the Colonel would have retired on one if it had been possible.

"I've been commissioned by a family to paint a portrait of their late father. He was a major in the army, close to promotion when he died. The family has given me bundles of photos, but he always appears stiff, in his military posture. The candids aren't much better. I've always been able to meet with the subjects of my portraits, get a sense of who they are, which of course is impossible in this case. I'd like to speak to your dad, observe him if possible, get the sense of a military man to help learn the essence of one. Most veterans in Rosewood weren't career soldiers and are not at the same rank."

"But not all colonels are similar in nature," Olivia responded. "My dad's…pretty formal."

"If you'd rather I didn't—"

"It's not that. I'm afraid you won't get much from him. He lived and breathed army."

Kate's eyebrows shot up. "That's a plus. The family pretty much described their father the same way. Do you think you could get me an introduction?"

Olivia blinked. "He's not active military anymore. You can just talk to him, no red tape to get through."

"No, but he wasn't responsive when I phoned. I'm hoping if you asked, he might cooperate."

She should have known. "The Colonel's comfort zone begins and ends with the military. But if you think it would help, I'll ask."

"That would be amazing." Kate brushed back her auburn hair and smiled. "I feel terrible having come here originally to ask a favor."

"Originally?"

"Unless you'd rather I not, I'd like to be a friend, not just someone who passes you on the sidewalk."

Touched, Olivia smiled. "I'd like that, too." For the first time since she had been a small child, Olivia realized she could have a friend, one she didn't have to bid goodbye in a matter of months.

Chapter Three

Deciding that Joey was going to remain silent, Zeke headed out the door of the clinic with the boy in tow, pausing to point out the buildings. "You can see that's the barn. The stables. And the corral's off that way. I'll show you the lay of the land later. Chores are waiting."

The two-story barn was meticulously clean, fragrant with the aroma of fresh hay. Zeke never could decide which he liked better, the comfort of his home or the warm feeling of the barn. His own cow, Milkdud, which he'd raised since she'd been a sickly calf, mooed in welcome. Adjoining stalls held various recovering domestic stock that required daily care.

Zeke introduced the assortment. Three horses, two cows, three pigs and four sheep. The new patients were stabled in the front stalls. After making some notes, Zeke headed back to his office. Joey trailed behind, surreptitiously checking out the grounds and other buildings. Zeke hid a grin. His little ranch wasn't any Disneyland, but it was a lot more interesting to a twelve-year-old than school.

Once back inside, Zeke checked blood results with Angie. Glancing up, Zeke noticed that Joey had wandered over to the aquarium. But this time he kept his arms at his sides, not touching the glass, just watching the fish. Quick learner.

"Angie, how many appointments this afternoon?"

She looked at the computer screen. "Besides the puff-ball, not too many." They'd had to make up appointments they had canceled the day before with the chick debacle.

"We should be okay, then." Zeke strolled over to Joey, wanting to know more about this boy who had never been allowed a pet other than a turtle. "Joey, while Angie's prepping the first patient, watch the phones."

Joey spun around, his eyes wide. "And answer them?"

Zeke thought of Olivia's delayed reaction when the chicks had first scattered. Definitely related to his mother. "Yes."

"But I don't know what to say."

"Answer 'Harrison Veterinary.' If it's routine, take a message. If it's an emergency, come get Angie or me."

His eyes grew even bigger. "How do I know if it's an emergency?"

Zeke smiled to himself. The boy wasn't as indifferent as he pretended. "Most people know when it's serious and they'll tell you. If they don't know, ask one of us."

Joey's Adam's apple rose up and down as he visibly swallowed.

Zeke pointed to a few labels on the multibutton phone. "Our beeper and cell numbers are marked." He lifted a spindle from the desk. "Messages go here."

The boy ran nervous hands down the legs of his jeans.

"If you're sure it's an emergency, beep us with the number 911." He pointed again to the phone. "It's preset right here."

Joey gingerly sat in the chair behind the desk. Heading to the barn, Zeke mentally ticked off the afternoon's procedures, all routine: one case of bovine mastitis, a split hoof, some mild colic and an infected ear. Just one horse had him concerned.

Zeke patted the filly, confident about the ultimate outcome. "She'll be fine."

"Thanks, Doc," the grateful owner responded.

Zeke stroked the horse's silky mane. "And you stay away from milkweed, my friend." The words barely out, his beeper went off.

911.

"Mom!" Joey yanked the phone out of Olivia's hand.

Zeke burst through the door on a dead run into the clinic.

"There's no emergency," Joey rushed to explain, glaring up at his mother.

Olivia winced. "Joey was showing me the beeper on the phone and I accidentally pushed the preset button." Zeke's face filled with disbelief.

And Olivia didn't blame him a bit. "I'm really sorry. I seem to fumble everything these days." The man must think she was an absolute idiot.

"Better to find out it wasn't an emergency," he replied, releasing a whoosh of relief. "Not that I'd encourage any more false alarms."

"Of course not." She flushed, her face hot. "Um, I hope this won't be counted against Joey. For his community service."

Zeke turned toward Joey. "What do you think? Should we let her off?"

Joey smirked. "I'd have to do more volunteer work."

Zeke scrunched his brow in concentration. "I think you've got something there."

Olivia blinked. "You're not serious?"

"You *did* push the 911 button."

She looked at Zeke, then Joey. "Fine. Do you want me to start tonight or will tomorrow morning be soon enough?"

Zeke stroked his firm jaw, appearing to deliberate. "Morning ought to be soon enough."

"I'll wear my jeans and an old T-shirt."

Grinning, Zeke started to speak when the door opened and a rush of perfume and yapping pushed inside. Zeke's benign smile disappeared and Olivia could see a tic in his clenched jaw.

"Belinda," Zeke said curtly to the woman.

Olivia looked over, hoping she hid her surprise. The woman was decked out in designer clothes she would have expected to see in Houston's Galleria or on Rodeo Drive in Beverly Hills, but not in little Rosewood. Although she hadn't visited veterinary clinics herself, Olivia guessed most people didn't dress for their appointments the way this woman did.

Angie pushed open the door and made her way to the desk. "You can have a seat, Belinda. The doctor will see you in a few minutes."

Her eyebrows raised at Angie's brisk instructions, Belinda frowned at a chair, then perched on its edge as though not wanting to muss her expensive clothes. The dog sat beside her, its glittering collar and leash seeming glaringly out of place.

Olivia hadn't seen anyone like this woman in Rosewood, and it was all she could do not to stare.

Zeke took her elbow.

Surprised, Olivia forced herself to act casual.

He walked her to the door and seemed preoccupied as they stepped outside.

Olivia cleared a nervous knot in her throat. "So, Joey, you about ready to head home?"

Joey glanced at Zeke for approval.

Surprised, Olivia was at a loss for words. Lately Joey had barely acknowledged the need for approval from anyone.

Zeke agreed, "Works for me. Get here early tomorrow and I'll make buckwheat pancakes."

"With maple syrup?" Joey questioned, as though she never cooked pancakes for him.

"Warm maple syrup," Zeke promised.

Olivia tried to regain a little control. "That's not necessary."

Zeke shrugged. "I have a taste for them, so I'll be up early cooking."

Clearly she was outnumbered. Having worried about Joey all day, Olivia was taken aback to see that he was handling the entire situation better than she was.

"I'm curious." Zeke drew his dark eyebrows together in contemplation. "Just when did Joey call you?"

"Well…"

"He was with me out in the barn earlier for a few hours. He came back inside to relieve Angie on the phones…what, five minutes before you pressed the emergency beeper? It raises the question, how did you get out here from town before Joey had time to call you?"

Squirming inwardly, Olivia searched for an explanation that wouldn't mortify her son. Yes, he was twelve now, but he was still her baby. One she worried about constantly now that Ted was gone. It was as though Joey was now even more vulnerable, more susceptible to anything that could harm him.

Her worry wasn't grounded in fact, but having experienced how quickly a life could be snatched away… Joey should be safe in Rosewood, probably safer than anywhere else. And the veterinary clinic was hardly a dangerous place, but it didn't dampen her concern. Overprotective, the Colonel was always saying. So much so that he thought she wasn't raising Joey right, not disciplining him as she should.

"Mom?" Joey stared at her, his face scrunched in question.

Olivia shook her head. "Sorry. Zeke, do you want Joey to stay longer today? I can come back later."

Zeke's usual cheerfulness was absent as he studied her quizzically. "No need. He put in enough time for today."

"In that case, Joey can use the rest of the afternoon to do his school assignments." Feeling oddly out of step, as though the rest of the world were revolving just a minute or so faster than she was, Olivia clutched her keys.

"See you in the morning," Zeke replied quietly.

"Okay," she agreed.

Watching her leave, Zeke concentrated more on her face than her form. Not that she wasn't just as attractive, but the haunting vulnerability in her eyes struck him. In those few moments she'd looked as though something awful was about to happen. Having lost her husband was terrible enough. What could be worse?

"Zeke?" Angie prodded, having followed him outside.

He exhaled. "Sorry, long day."

"Once you see Her Highness, we can take a break."

Sighing, Zeke forced himself to turn around. Maybe Angie was right. It was about time Belinda took her dog to another vet. He didn't need a living reminder. Like a pebble in his shoe, Belinda was a memory he couldn't ignore.

Apparently feeling protective, Angie didn't leave his side while he examined Fluffy.

Belinda practically purred as she spoke. And he didn't imagine the satisfaction in her eyes.

Once she and Fluffy were gone, Angie threw open a

window. "That woman wears enough perfume for half the town."

There had been a time when he'd saved up all his allowance and most of what he made at his after-school job to buy her perfume. Not the expensive one she was wearing. Come to think of it, he didn't remember her ever wearing the perfume he had bought her. His bulb had been dim, blind and deaf. "How's the appointment book looking, Angie?"

"Good news on that front. We're caught up. Just had a cancellation for our last appointment. Except for our resident menagerie, we can pack it in for today."

Rubbing the back of his neck, he listened with only half an ear. "Go on home, Angie. I'll take care of the stock."

"But what about the kennel and—"

"I can use the time with our patients."

She studied him for a moment. "And I can use the time to catch up at home. See you tomorrow."

"Right." His mind full, he wandered outside, stopping first at the brooder. Olivia immediately came to mind. She'd been something, chasing down that flock of scattering chicks. Checking, he saw the brooder's temperature was high enough for the baby chickens. There weren't as many chicks as usual, since he'd taken the infamous batch to the 4-H club. Vehemently opposed to the sickening conditions of many commercial chicken-and-egg producers, he had a small operation of free-range chickens. And the chicks were always in demand by the locals.

Hearing a pickup truck traveling up the long driveway, he poked his head outside and recognized his father's old Chevy. Robert Harrison could afford a new one but claimed it wouldn't have the *personality* of his well-worn vehicle.

Zeke carefully secured the brooder, then raised a hand in greeting, always glad to see his father.

Robert climbed from the cab of the truck, still agile and active although he was in his late sixties now. "You in the middle of something?"

"Nope. Just checking on the residents. And I was thinking I ought to make a fresh pot of coffee."

"Reminds me." Robert reached back into the cab of the truck. "Your mother sent some stew and half a chocolate-fudge cake. Says I'll finish off the cake if it's in our kitchen."

Zeke grinned, much of his Belinda-induced fatigue fading. "Good thing I'm hungry. Might just have to eat some of that cake. Only polite to share."

It didn't take long to get the coffee brewing and pull out plates for cake. He stuck the plastic bowl of stew in the microwave.

"You *are* hungry."

"Just one of those days, Dad. Playing catch-up on some missed appointments." His father knew the nature of the business made that fairly common. After he sliced a hefty chunk of cake for his father and emptied his now-warm stew into a stoneware bowl, Zeke filled him in on Olivia and the chick debacle.

Robert was laughing before Zeke finished the story. "Too bad you didn't get that on video."

Zeke speared a wedge of potato. "They were moving too fast for me to think about anything except catching them."

"Coffee's done." Robert got up and filled the two mugs sitting on the counter. He put the mugs on the table and then grabbed a carton of cream from the fridge. "Now I can dig into that cake."

Concentrating on the stew, Zeke finished it before lifting his own mug.

"You'd better eat at least as much cake as I do. Beats me how, but your mother will know if I get the lion's share."

"Don't have to twist my arm." Zeke cut a healthy piece for himself and started eating it with the same enthusiasm he'd had for the stew.

Robert watched him for a few moments. "How long since you've eaten?"

"Breakfast. Like I said, really crammed schedule."

"From the chicken woman," Robert noted. "Which messed up yesterday's appointments. Nothing serious while you were gone?"

"Nope."

"Doesn't sound like she meant to cause any trouble."

"Nah. It was an accident. Good thing." Remembering, he shook his head, unable to suppress a grin. "Hate to think what she could have done if she *was* trying."

Chuckling, Robert reached for another bite of cake. "Sounds like someone worth getting to know."

Zeke remembered the look in her eyes before she left with Joey. "Why?"

"She sure wouldn't be dull."

"And with my track record, I need someone more like the chicken woman?"

"Son, you've got to let go of the past. You were a kid when you met Belinda. And by college she'd…I'll be kind and say *changed*. It's best that you found out her true colors before marriage."

Zeke snorted. "You forgetting that she refused to marry me? Wasn't my choice."

"Doesn't matter. You're still better off." Robert paused, his fork midair. "You don't still have feelings for Belinda, do you?"

"No. Can't see now why I ever did."

Robert exhaled. "That's a relief. I was beginning to think I'd never see you get married."

"Well, don't get out the rice just yet. Still don't trust my judgment enough to marry someone. Look at Penny—I couldn't figure out she was still in love with her ex-husband."

Frowning, Robert put his fork down. "You loved Penny's kids more than her."

"You just made my case, Dad. I don't have good sense when it comes to women."

"But, son, you're going to be wind up lonely—"

Zeke held up one hand. "First off, with a family our size, I'll never be lonely. And I date, Dad. You married the best woman on the planet and now the pickings are way too slim."

"You telling me that of all the women you've dated since college, you haven't been tempted?"

Just with Penny. Considering the children, going back with her ex was the best outcome for her. But it had re-inforced his certainty that when it came to relationships, his judgment was flat-out bad. Otherwise, he would have realized that she'd still loved her ex. Zeke shook his head. "Just not in the cards for me, Dad. I'll leave marriage to the experts like you and Mom."

"We'd like to see you settled with a woman who has a heart as good as yours."

Embarrassed at the praise, Zeke pushed it aside. "One who wants to take in every stray like I do?" Remembering, he softened his voice. "Like you and Mom when you took me in?"

"Best thing we ever did." Robert cleared his throat. "We want to make sure you *stay* happy."

Those first months as their foster kid, he'd driven his new family well beyond the edge of their patience and then some, but they never gave up on him. "Dad, I'm happy." He gestured out the window at the acres of land his small ranch encompassed, the well-kept outbuildings and barn that allowed him to practice as he wanted. "Look at all I have. Wouldn't have happened without your guidance."

"And *your* hard work," his father insisted. "We still got the best end of the deal." Robert swallowed the last bite of his cake. "You think any of your brothers or sisters would have shared this?"

"Mom's cake is worth tussling over."

"So, you haven't told me."

Puzzled, Zeke looked at him in question.

"About the woman who scattered your brood."

"I told you what happened."

His father's eyes remained steady. "But not about her."

Zeke raised his eyebrows. "I'm guessing right now her life is as scattered as those chicks were."

"That all you noticed about her?"

Zeke hadn't forgotten the jolt of sensation when she'd accidentally grabbed his hands or the vulnerability in her unusual violet eyes. "She's got plenty of troubles without adding me to the mix."

"Hmm." Robert glanced at the remaining cake.

Smiling, Zeke cut another wedge and placed it on his father's plate.

"Too bad," Robert continued. "She sounds like a corker. Nothing better than a woman with spunk."

Chapter Four

"That's not one of your *old* T-shirts." Joey paused at the entrance of the clinic.

Olivia nudged him forward. "Concentrate on your work, not me." Still, she tugged at the tail of her lavender T-shirt, hoping it wouldn't look new to Zeke. Technically it wasn't new. She'd bought it weeks ago; she just hadn't worn it before.

"I smell pancakes," Joey announced. "If I gotta come here, let's eat." The door to the private quarters was fully open. Not hesitating, he trotted past the doorway. Seemed hunger had trumped rebellion. In moments he'd disappeared.

Olivia felt far more uncertain.

"Come on in," Zeke hollered from somewhere in the back.

Joey had probably already reached the kitchen, but Olivia wasn't as confident, certainly not as bold. Clearly a man's home, the room held a large well-used leather chair the color of mahogany—much like most of the wood pieces, including the crowded bookcase and the side tables filled with veterinary magazines. A tall, wide fireplace dominated one wall. Unlit because of the warm temperatures, the imposing hearth proclaimed its prominence with raw, rough-hewn granite. Wide-planked oak floors creaked slightly beneath her feet as she trod inside.

She could envision Zeke, his long legs stretched out so that his boots rested on the scarred coffee table, face buried in one of the hundreds of books.

"Mom!" Joey appeared, looking annoyed. "Zeke says if you want to eat, come on."

Wondering if that was a direct quote, Olivia answered him. "Okay." Following her sure-footed son, she lagged behind. Venturing into yet another strange place reminded her of all the new schools she'd had to enter each time her father had been transferred, the stares of the other kids, none of whom would remain longtime friends, because she would have moved on again before that could happen.

A spatula in his right hand, Zeke pointed with the other to a coffeepot. "Just brewed. Hope you like it strong."

She spotted a mug rack and took one emblazoned with a Texas A&M logo, the university with the best veterinary program in the state. No doubt Zeke's alma mater.

"Cream's in the fridge," Zeke told her, flipping a pancake. "Sugar's on the table."

"I want milk. I can get the cream," Joey offered, clearly already acquainted with the kitchen. "They're on the same shelf."

"We use the kitchen for a break room during work hours, so Joey was in here yesterday," Zeke explained. "Gives me more space on the other side for supplies and indoor kenneling."

"Kenneling?"

"Small animals I've operated on that need to stay through the night." He flipped another pancake. "For observation."

"So you have someone who works the night shift?"

Zeke shook his head.

"Then who watches the overnight animals?"

"I have an intercom and I'm a light sleeper."

Joey shoved a small carton of cream at her. Accepting it, she didn't pour any into her cup. Early as it was, Zeke looked like a mass of energy despite any nighttime interruptions.

"Joey, you'd better throw a few plates on the table so we can eat," Zeke instructed as he added another pancake to the growing stack.

She tried not to wince. Apparently Zeke didn't remember that young boys often took comments literally. "Hope you don't mind paper towels," Zeke continued, grabbing a roll and plopping it on the table. "Don't have many dinner guests."

"It's breakfast," Joey pointed out.

"So it is." Reaching back, Zeke grabbed a platter. "Silverware's in the far left drawer." He lifted his sturdy shoulders in a half shrug. "My mother says I have the whole kitchen set up backward."

Olivia found her voice. "As long as it works for you."

"I can only cook three things. She takes pity on me and sends over leftovers. And Angie brings in more food than I can eat."

To her surprise, Olivia wondered if there was a yet-unmentioned girlfriend in the mix. She'd gotten the idea yesterday that he was single, but that was just an assumption. "You really didn't have to make breakfast for us."

"Just stirred up more batter. I was going to make pancakes anyway."

Trying not to feel like an outsider as she had most of her life, Olivia put her mug on the table. "Can I do something to help?"

"Syrup's in the microwave. You can grab that."

Grateful for something to busy herself with, Olivia looked around the good-size kitchen and spotted the microwave. She never bothered to heat the syrup. She'd always thought that was something they just did in restaurants. She reached for the small bottle. Not thinking that it would be too hot, she jerked back at the heat on the glass container. The action splashed a small bit of the red-hot syrup on her hand. Brought up to never moan over what the Colonel termed a "small incident," she didn't say anything, instead looked for the sink.

Zeke turned around, sized up the situation and grabbed her good hand. "Thought you knew it'd be hot." Leading her to the sink, he shook his head. "It's like jam or filled doughnuts—they get hot as a greased pit in the microwave."

"I can—"

But Zeke was already turning on the faucet. He quickly put her injured hand under the cool stream of water. "Joey, grab a big bowl from the hutch."

"Hutch?"

"The big piece of furniture over there. Bowls are on the bottom shelf."

"There's no need to fuss—" Olivia began.

"Who's fussing? Good grief, woman, you want a blister?"

"Of course not." But it was hard to argue with him as he gently touched her hand, careful to make sure the water pressure wasn't too forceful, that the reddened skin was handled with care. It had been so long since her hand had been held by a man. Or since she'd stood so close…

"This one okay?" Joey asked.

Startled, Olivia jerked her hand back, putting too much pressure on the burn.

Zeke's puzzlement showed in his face, but he didn't

comment in front of Joey, instead taking the bowl and filling it with cold water.

To cover her flub, Olivia started to turn to the refrigerator. "I'll get some ice."

"No. That'll just aggravate the burn. The cool water will keep the reddening down, and while your hand's in the water, the air can't get to it and make it hurt more. Then we'll cut open a stalk of aloe vera, rub it on the welt and it'll be good as new in a day."

"Oh." Well, he was a doctor, even though he worked on patients of the four-footed variety....

As though to contest her thoughts, she heard squawking from another room.

"Dilbert," Zeke explained. "My parrot. Every now and then he decides to try to fly, then smacks into the furniture."

"Why can't he fly?"

"Wing damage."

"And he just roams around free?" Instantly she imagined the amount of bird droppings.

"No, but he can pick locks better than most thieves. I'll round him up after breakfast and put him back in his cage."

"Why can't he just walk around outside and not be in a cage?" Joey asked with a scowl.

"Because he'd wind up as somebody's dinner. He doesn't have any defenses and he wouldn't be able to escape if a predator took after him. Coyotes, eagles."

Still not looking mollified, Joey continued to scowl. "How'd he hurt his wing?"

Zeke shrugged. "Don't know."

"How come?" Joey demanded.

"Joey—" Olivia began.

"It's okay. Somebody found him hurt in Fredericksburg. I got a call and, well, he's been here ever since."

Olivia frowned, as well. "Aren't there veterinarians in Fredericksburg?"

"Of course. But not all of them have the space I do. People know I take in strays." The bowl was now nearly full and Zeke took her hand and guided it into the water. "Keep it covered. Now, we'd better eat those pancakes before they turn into Frisbees. 'Course, if they're cold, that hot syrup ought to warm them up."

Olivia swallowed, wondering if he was being sarcastic.

"And since your mom risked…well, not life, but certainly limb, we ought to dig in." He looked over at Olivia, not a trace of sarcasm or meanness in his expression. "Right- or left-handed?"

"Right."

"Good thing the burn's on your left, then."

Well, if Zeke didn't think she was a hopeless klutz from the lost-chicks episode the day before, he must now. Awkwardly she placed the bowl on the table beside one of the plates. Perhaps for an encore she could dump coffee in her lap.

"How many pancakes, Olivia?"

"One, thanks."

Zeke's eyebrows rose. "Not too confident about my cooking?"

"No." Flustered, she stirred the water in the bowl with her fingers. "I mean, I'm not all that hungry."

Tilting his head in the direction of the fully stacked platter, he sent her a look of disapproval. "Better eat more than one."

"She doesn't eat much anymore," Joey commented, digging into his own pancakes.

The innocent but painful reminder made her freeze.

Silence filled the room. Only the scraping of Joey's fork against the plate as he ate interrupted the quiet.

Zeke met her gaze, his eyes filled with questions and a touch of sympathy.

Olivia bowed her head.

But Zeke's intense perusal didn't waver.

Swallowing, she tried to pick up her fork—anything to distract herself and him. Forgetting the bowl of water, she lifted that hand as well, splashing water on the table.

"Watch it!" Joey complained. "You're getting water on my pancakes!"

Zeke tossed him a paper towel. "You'll live."

Joey rolled his eyes.

No doubt her son was thinking how unfair it was that there were two sets of rules, one for adults, one for kids, Olivia realized. But certainly more compelling was the look in Zeke's eyes. She didn't want pity. Was there something more in his gaze? Something that didn't reside in that sorrowful tier of emotions?

Ted had been the center of her life, the anchor that had begun to make her believe she could belong. Just like anyone else. That she wasn't destined to always be an outsider. When he died, all that had disappeared.

And it would take far more than a disarming veterinarian with unforgettable blue eyes for her to recover.

Chapter Five

"Hold still," Zeke ordered.

Squirming in a chair in the exam room, Olivia tried again to pull her burned hand away. "It's fine. I don't need anything on it."

"Aloe vera straight from the plant. Can't believe you never tried it for burns."

"I'm not a native Texan," she replied, still trying to inch backward. "They don't usually pull out thorny plants at an army infirmary to treat wounds."

"Humor me." Man, she was prickly. You'd think he was trying to amputate instead of prevent blisters. "Why don't you go home, wait a few days till this heals to help around here?"

Her already-perfect posture squared into a frame that rivaled a ballroom dancer's. "I'm not a fragile china doll. I've finished a hike with a fractured ankle, ridden the rapids with a pulled shoulder and walked five miles after a snakebite. A little hot syrup's not going to stop me."

"Impressive. I thought it was your dad who was in the army. Sounds like you trained for Special Forces."

"That's what army families are," she admitted, then

snapped her mouth closed, uncomfortable with the admission.

He deftly wrapped a nonstick pad with self-adhering gauze to her hand, covering the reddened skin. "I imagine it goes with being in the military."

"You can't begin to imagine moving from place to place without any notice, barely time to say goodbye, never knowing where you'll end up."

Zeke's caustic snort remained inside. No, how would he know what it was like to be bounced from home to home?

She sighed, running her other hand through her honey-blond hair. "Sorry. It's one of my easily pushed buttons, the army-brat experience. And I'm so worried about Joey. Ever since his dad died…" She shrugged, a halfhearted motion that lifted only one shoulder. "I fell apart. If my parents hadn't held things together, I'd hate to think how much worse our situation could be. But Joey and I…" She paused, the seconds passing slowly, so slowly he could hear the neighing of horses in the corral, the low meowing of cats in the next room. "Joey and I have always had such a close bond. Ted was his hero, but I'm the one who baked cookies for him after school, bandaged scraped knees, made his peanut-butter-and-jelly sandwiches…" She trailed off.

Zeke remained silent, guessing she needed to talk.

"I never expected Joey to act like he has. Now he won't talk to me." Olivia's head snapped up, her face drawn in dismay. "I didn't mean to dump all this on you. Point is, I'm tougher than I look." She pulled her hand back. "And I can do my fair share of work around here." She held up her now-bandaged hand. "No special consideration needed."

There was plenty of determination in her violet eyes but so much wariness he wondered which would win. "If you insist that you're okay to work, you can start with walking the patients in post-op."

Olivia frowned. "Dogs? You want me to walk dogs? That's not work."

"Here it is. Getting them moving is part of the recuperation process."

She looked dubious.

"Just like people who've had surgery." Zeke stood, placing the first-aid kit on a lower shelf, then made himself not smile when he turned around. "What were you expecting to do on the first day? Surgery? Deliver a calf? Or something simple like drawing blood?"

Olivia didn't look amused.

Puzzled, Zeke drew his eyebrows together. "Lighten up. We get enough serious stuff to worry about here. And the dogs and cats in post-op are confused and miss their owners. It's important enough."

Olivia's expression softened. "Of course. I wasn't thinking." Again she twisted her blond hair around one finger.

Morning light pooled through the window and he had an immediate desire to reach out and see if Olivia's hair was as soft as it looked.

"You're the boss," she continued with an impish glint to her expression. "I'd love to walk dogs." Her smile suddenly disappeared. "But what if they don't like me?"

"Why shouldn't they?"

"Well, I don't know anything about animals and I've read they can sense that."

Zeke chuckled. "Then it's a good thing you're not walking lions or tigers. Come on, let's get started."

Olivia looked out the window to where Joey was helping Angie with the morning feed.

"Joey's fine." Zeke pushed the rolling stool back to its usual corner, then opened the connecting door to the kennels. "Each animal has a chart. You note when you take him out and when you return. Also any output."

"Output?" She pinkened, then cleared her throat. "Oh, of course."

"We'll start you out with a dog who had routine surgery and is doing well." He pointed toward a back wall. "That's our ICU. All of their exercise is closely monitored, and either Angie or I will work with them."

She turned to the back wall. "I only see one dog and a cat."

"Thankfully. I like it best when it's empty."

Olivia nodded in agreement. "Of course. Just trying to take everything in."

And she was. From the feeding stations to the surgical equipment to the small assortment of kenneled animals.

Zeke stopped at the first crate. They were built so that if needed, one animal could be held in the top portion, a second in the bottom. He liked it best when they were at eye level. Pets were less likely to get agitated when they could see their surroundings. He unfastened the crate so that the soft-eyed cocker spaniel could be retrieved. "This is Scratches."

Olivia's eyes widened. "I suppose that's better than Bites."

He chuckled. "She likes having her ears scratched. I don't see many Fidos or Spots."

"That's good," she replied with a wry twist of her lips. "Seeing spots wouldn't be very good in your occupation."

Laughing at the pun, Zeke snapped on a leash, then lifted the dog gently from the thickly padded bed. "Hey, Scratches. You need to escape?"

The golden-colored dog licked his hand affectionately. Zeke carried her past the wall of crates so he wouldn't stir up his other patients. He pushed open the door to a large grassy patch, set Scratches down and handed Olivia the leash.

Gingerly accepting it, she looked at him for directions. For the life of him, Zeke couldn't recall another time when he'd had to explain how to walk a dog. "Give Scratches her lead."

Olivia looked at him blankly.

"Let her start walking and keep up with her. The pickup bags are on the post and there's a can next to it for disposal. Check each chart. Some have to be collected for testing."

She stared at him.

"You don't throw those Baggies away."

"Oh." Not looking thrilled at this part, Olivia walked cautiously behind Scratches, who sniffed at the grass.

Zeke pointed in the direction of the barn. "Walk her about ten minutes now. This afternoon she should be up to twenty. Angie will show you how to chart the dog's progress. If they're wobbly, energetic, specific behavior."

"Then what?"

"Why don't we start with exercising them for now? Don't give them treats unless the chart specifically states no food restrictions."

"Who usually does this?" Olivia asked.

"Whoever's available. Angie, me, a volunteer."

"Oh, do you have many volunteers?"

"Joey's not the only kid to get in trouble at school and be assigned community service."

Olivia digested this. "Is Joey doing all right?"

"It's only his second day."

She shook her head, unintentionally tugging the leash at the same time. "Oh, sorry, doggy."

"Scratches."

"Scratches," she repeated. "Is she in pain?"

"She's on Rimadyl. It helps."

"How do you know? I mean, they can't talk."

"How did you know what Joey wanted when he was a toddler? How he felt? When he was in pain?"

Olivia paused, memories softening her expression. "It's hard to verbalize, but their eyes… It's as though they speak."

"Pretty much the same for animals. You have to interpret expressions, behavior."

She stared up at him and he wondered what she hid in those incredible violet eyes.

The moment stretched out until Olivia cleared her throat. "How do I let you know if something's going wrong? I mean while I'm walking the pets."

Zeke reached into the pocket of his jeans and pulled out a coach's whistle. "This'll get my attention in a hurry, but we carry our cell phones, as well."

She tapped her pocket with her free hand. "I have mine."

"After you've walked Scratches, program in my number and Angie's." It gave him a little start to realize that he liked the idea of her having his phone number. "And I'll need your cell number, too. It's in the office, but I'd rather store it in my phone."

Nodding, she looked down at the dog. "I can't help wishing she *could* talk. Then if I mess up—"

"I haven't had anyone flunk pet walking yet."

Olivia sighed. "You just haven't met anyone like me."

Perhaps she was right. There wasn't anything about her that reminded him of a single other person, certainly not any other woman.

Still thinking far too much about Olivia, Zeke got to work on the day's appointments. And one of his more ornery patients, Ziggy the goat, was next. He also needed to get Joey more involved.

"Come on, Joey. The next patient is outside."

Rufe Goggins sat on a hay bale, holding Ziggy's lead. The goat eyed Zeke suspiciously even though they were well acquainted. Probably *because* they were acquainted. Ziggy associated Zeke with inoculations and checkups. Animals didn't have to talk for him to know what many were thinking.

"Joey, stand over there on that side of the goat." He waited until the boy complied. "So, Ziggy, what's got your goat today?"

Rufe hooted as he always did, which was why Zeke always used the worn greeting for Ziggy. "Something's got him twitchy, Doc. Can't tell what."

Ziggy was obstinate, single-minded and intelligent. But he wasn't twitchy by nature. Zeke pulled on gloves, then ran his hands over the goat's sides and belly. Nothing felt amiss. Ziggy didn't pull away but stamped his hooves in warning.

"There's something stuck in his leg," Joey piped up.

Surprised, Zeke turned to the boy.

Joey pointed at one of the goat's rear legs.

Zeke circled the goat, then squatted down. The tip of something small protruded. Looking closer, he was surprised to discover the object was metal. Carefully running his hands over the leg, he felt the barb, deeply embedded. "Rufe, good thing you know your animals so well. If this had stayed in, it could have become infected. He might have even lost a leg."

Rufe paled.

"I'll need an X-ray. Then I'll remove it."

"He's gonna be okay, though, Doc?" Rufe's casual pretense vanished.

Knowing how much Rufus valued the animal, Zeke

spoke to him reassuringly. "I don't foresee any problems, Rufe."

"Can I stay with him?" Rufe asked anxiously.

"Angie will schedule him as soon as we run the blood work. Barring an emergency, I'll get to Ziggy real quick." He looked over at the boy. "Good call, Joey."

He shrugged as usual.

But Zeke saw beyond the well-practiced gesture. "You did a great job. That's what counts."

Joey scuffed his shoe against the ground. "I was closer and I'm not as tall."

Ziggy turned his shaggy head, then nudged the boy. "Is he mad?" Joey stared uncertainly at the goat.

"Just the opposite."

Rufe scratched his smooth, shiny scalp. "Ain't that something? Ziggy don't take to strangers. Don't take to people he knows, either."

"Animals have good instincts," Zeke remarked.

Tentatively, Joey stretched out his hand.

Ziggy nudged it, swung his head back toward Rufe, then nudged Joey's hand again.

He was thanking the boy, Zeke realized. Joey might not have had much experience with animals, but he inspired trust in one of the most ornery patients Zeke had ever encountered. There was much more to this boy than the facade he had created. It wasn't much of a leap to remember his own protective shell at that age.

After checking the rest of his patients in the barn, Zeke headed back to his office.

"Angie, can you prep Ziggy for his X-ray?" The goat had to be calmed or he would struggle and kick through the process and they would end up with a blurred, useless image of something barely resembling a leg. "And book him for the first slot after we get his blood work processed."

"Is it bad?" Angie glanced up from the computer in concern.

"Joey spotted a barb in one of his rear legs. It's deep but since we caught it before infection, it should be textbook."

Angie eyebrows rose as her eyes signaled all kinds of questions. "Good going, Joey."

The boy remained silent as he turned toward the aquarium but for the first time didn't shrug. Progress. It came in tiny steps.

"Local anesthetic?" Angie questioned, needing to know exactly what to prep.

"Yep." Some goats didn't fare well under a general anesthetic, sometimes resulting in fatalities. And a local would do fine to get the X-ray.

Joey turned back around. "Uh, is Ziggy gonna be okay?"

"Yeah." Knowing any additional praise would only make the boy uncomfortable, Zeke kept his reply short. But this first spark of interest was a start.

Didn't take Angie long to draw a blood sample. He wanted to rule out infection even though no signs of one presented themselves.

As he'd suspected, Ziggy's blood work was fine, his white cell count normal. "Angie, will you prep Ziggy?" Angie shaved the area around the barb in record time.

Though he'd planned to have Joey sweep out the storeroom, Zeke impulsively changed his mind when Angie returned. As she settled back behind her desk, Zeke decided to give Joey a chance to see more than the inside of the office. He'd done well earlier that morning finding the barb in the goat's leg, and Zeke thought it might give the boy a shot of self-confidence to see the result. "Come on, Joey. Let's take a look at Ziggy."

The goat eyed them suspiciously when they entered the barn. Angie had set up his tray of instruments along with a syringe and Ziggy's updated statistics. The procedure was as sterile as a house call would have been. One glimpse told him the goat had maintained his weight, a good sign.

But Rufe was still hovering, more anxious than before. "He's not gonna like this."

Zeke was fairly certain the operation would bother Rufe more than Ziggy. But he understood all the aspects of loving and caring for animals, the link between them and their owners. In truth Ziggy was more a pet than domestic stock, although Rufe would never admit it. "We'll see."

Joey watched keenly while Zeke approached the animal.

"So, Ziggy, you know the procedure." With a firm hand, Zeke pushed on Ziggy's posterior, causing the animal to sit on its tailbone. Almost immediately, the goat started to relax. "Calms him down so I can administer the anesthetic and remove the barb," Zeke explained to Joey as he pointed toward the affected spot. "Angie's already shaved the immediate area."

Joey didn't take his eyes off the goat and Zeke's movements.

Zeke quickly injected the local anesthetic, then checked his watch. Wouldn't be long for it to take effect. After a short time, he tested the area, using a scalpel to cut a tiny slit. When Ziggy didn't react, Zeke was confident proceeding.

Removing the barb, he saw that it was serious. "Don't want to repeat myself, Joey, but this would have caused major problems if it had stayed in." He glanced over to make sure the incision and procedure weren't making the boy faint. Joey looked pale but intrigued. Not that it was a large incision. Rufe, however, wasn't faring as well. "Joey, head inside and watch the phones. Tell Angie to get Ziggy's meds ready and bring Rufe a hot cup of coffee with lots of sugar."

Nodding, Joey took off.

Zeke turned toward the goat's anxious owner. "Rufe, I'll wrap his leg and he'll be good to go."

"The old boy gets into the most peculiar stuff. Must have kicked the fence I'm working on," Rufe admitted, looking guilty.

"Keep him away from it until you're finished. I'll send you home with antibiotics, but the incision should heal quickly. And don't blame yourself. It's just his nature."

"Thanks, Doc."

Zeke patted the goat's flank. "And you stay away from metal fences, my friend."

Olivia noticed she and Joey were both getting used to the routine, even enjoying it. Returning home from a late-afternoon stop at the town beauty salon, Olivia had barely closed the door behind her when a beeper went off in the kitchen. Frowning, she wondered what was beeping. The stove?

Egad.

It was the slow-cooking ribs she had slid in the oven just before she and Joey had left that morning. After the long day, she'd completely forgotten that she had invited her parents for dinner. Wonderful. But it was a way to ease into asking her dad to speak with Kate.

She loved her parents to pieces, but the timing couldn't be worse. Joey would be in a sulk since she hadn't let him go to his friend's house, only to the library to research a science project. And her parents would see his mood first thing.

Olivia wished she hadn't taken time to stop at Hair By Beth. She always needed more time to prepare for the Colonel. A sheen of nervous perspiration began forming on her forehead. It had been this way since she was a kid. The truth was that her father had wanted a boy. Not only was she a girl, but she never had been able to flourish under her father's military authority. The Colonel had always termed it her "lack of willpower." Forgetful, sometimes whimsical, she had her head in the clouds, he said, and she needed to get it back to the real world.

Olivia sighed. As though the real world had been such a good alternative. After spending the next two hours preparing appetizers and biscuits, she frowned when she finally heard Joey come home. She grabbed a towel and wiped her hands as she walked to the living room. "Joey, why are you so late?"

He shrugged.

"It's almost six!"

He shrugged again.

"And your grandparents are coming for dinner."

"So?"

Olivia winced. "I don't want to hear that tone in your voice again. We'll talk about this later. Get washed up and change your shirt."

He glanced down at his rumpled T-shirt. "How come?"

"Just change it, honey. You had it on at the clinic and it shows. Wash up and wear the shirt Grandma got you last week. She'll like seeing you in it."

Joey rolled his eyes in twelve-year-old bafflement but headed to his room.

Olivia checked on the biscuits. Luckily, she'd baked a lemon-meringue pie that morning. It was her father's favorite, and hopefully, it would keep him distracted.

* * *

Barely an hour later, she realized that lemon-meringue pie had only so much distracting ability. And the throbbing in her head was escalating with each passing minute.

"I'll make some fresh coffee." Olivia picked up the carafe, glad of an excuse to get away from the table and take some aspirin. Their small home didn't have a separate dining room, but the square black table was situated at the far end of the kitchen. Since her headaches were more frequent these days, Olivia kept a bottle of aspirin tucked in one of the kitchen cabinets. Turning on the water, she reached for a glass. She swallowed two aspirin, then filled the coffee basket with a mild blend that wouldn't keep her up all night.

As the brew dripped into the glass carafe, Olivia carried some more cream to the table.

"What do you mean, you have to miss baseball practice?" her father, Gerald Olson, asked Joey.

Her son took a gulp of milk to avoid answering.

"Joey says he won't be able to go to baseball practice, Olivia." The Colonel frowned up at her. "Why not?"

Great. Perhaps her head would just pop clean off her shoulders and be done with it. "He has community-service work to do instead."

The Colonel scowled. "You know it's Little League season. Why did you sign him up for community service?"

"There's nothing wrong with volunteer work," her mother commented mildly.

"That's not what I asked."

Mona Olson lifted her eyebrows, signaling there was nothing else she could do to douse the fire. She knew her husband well enough to recognize when he wouldn't be deterred.

"Joey's working at a veterinary clinic in lieu of being expelled."

The silence before the roar was ominous.

"Expelled?"

"Yes, Dad. He's been ditching classes and then one more—" Olivia paused, not wanting to tell her parents that Joey had been caught stealing "—event. It took a lot to keep him in school."

"If you had listened to me," Gerald began, "and sent him to Allegheny Prep—"

"Joey's not going to military school." The pit in Olivia's stomach nearly equaled the throbbing in her head. "I've already told you that." It had been her father's unrelenting suggestion each and every time Joey had gotten in trouble. She had argued against sending him away, not that the Colonel listened to her.

Her father scowled, his voice raising in volume and agitation. "Instead he's going to work at some vet's? Miss baseball season? What about his education? The discipline he needs?"

"Well, if he goes to military school, he won't be playing baseball," she retorted.

"Joey, would you show me your turtle?" Mona asked, getting up from the table.

Joey looked at his grandmother, then his mother. "Sure."

They were barely out of earshot when the Colonel took up his cause. "A boy raised without a man in the house is a boy headed for trouble."

Olivia blinked against a smarting of tears. "It wasn't a choice."

Her father sighed. "You know that's not what I meant. But you've got to think about Joey's future. Now he's skipping school. What's he going to be doing when he's eighteen?"

She swallowed the crowding lump of emotions in her throat. "Having trouble now doesn't mean he's going to do worse things. He just needs…time."

"He needs guidance. He'll get that at Allegheny Prep." True to his third-generation military background, her father didn't believe in pampering. Their home had been run on a strict schedule tempered only by her mother's soft touch.

"No, Dad. He's already lost one parent. I'm not going to make him feel like he's lost another by sending him away."

"What happens the next time he gets in trouble?"

She wished her father had the same faith in Joey that she did. "Are you so sure he's going to?"

"Afraid so."

"Dad, you know I appreciate all the support you and Mom have given us since Ted…" Her head and heart both ached. "I'm still in uncharted territory. That doesn't mean I won't get a grip on things."

"Olivia, you've always been naive, thinking everything would be all right just because you wished it to be. That's not reality. It's not raising a boy alone."

"Just because he's a boy doesn't mean I can't handle Joey."

"You're soft, like your mother. Coddle Joey and you'll have even bigger problems."

"I didn't exactly turn out to be a juvenile delinquent because of Mom's softness."

"And my guidelines," he reminded her.

"What about all the time you were gone on deployment? I didn't come unglued."

A flash of unexpected hurt surfaced in his eyes.

Immediately, Olivia clasped his hand. "Dad, I always knew you were only a letter or phone call away, that what you were doing was for us, for the country."

"You can't say the same for Joey."

"He has your genes, Dad. They balance out Mom's and my soft ones."

Her father shook his head. "Olivia, I'm saying what I believe is best for both of you. If you really want Joey to grow into a good man, you have to take steps now. You'd see him on holidays and in the summer."

New pain scorched a path from her heart to the pit in her stomach. She couldn't imagine anything worse. She was so lonely now she could barely stand it.

"There's something else I want to talk to you about, Dad."

"Don't tell me you've been up to mischief?" he teased, something that was rare.

She managed a small laugh. "Actually, I met an artist, Kate—"

"Artist?" His eyebrows pinched together in bemused disapproval.

"Yes, she's a very acclaimed painter. Her commissions come from museums all over the world." Olivia had looked up her new friend on Google and was awestruck that the down-to-earth woman was so well-known. "Her current project is from the Museum of Fine Arts in Houston."

The Colonel's eyes darkened in speculation.

"She's been commissioned to paint the portrait of a deceased army major. He was set to become a colonel when he died. Kate would like to meet with you—" Olivia lifted one shoulder "—to learn what makes a colonel a colonel so she can paint the finest rendition possible."

"Don't they usually do that from photos?"

"Some artists," Olivia admitted. "But Kate wants the essence of the man, and she can't get that from pictures. So would you meet with her?"

It was rare she asked him for a favor. And he knew it. "If it means all that much to you."

"Thanks, Dad. Kate will get in touch with you." Shoving back her chair, she got up from the table. "I'm going to pop into Joey's room, see if he or Mom wants more pie."

Her mother was still making a fuss over Joey's turtle. "When I was a girl, everyone had tiny turtles. Found out later they spread all kinds of bacteria, but I still thought mine was cute."

Joey carefully placed the turtle back in the grass-lined box. "Yeah, he's okay."

Olivia knew Joey wanted a pet he could play with, and he had always begged for a dog or cat. By no stretch of the imagination could this hard-shelled tortoise be considered a cuddly playmate.

She thought back to when she was eight years old and a friend had offered her a puppy, a mixed breed that was the color of glossy caramel. But her father had sternly refused. It had hurt more than the other times because she had already named him Carmie.

Maybe now that they were working at a veterinary practice, it would be possible. She was already learning more about animals. Hopefully, soon she could help Joey choose the right one.

Her mom looked over Joey's head, concern etched in her kind blue eyes. "Did your dad get enough coffee?"

Olivia looked down, knowing it wasn't coffee her mother meant. "Not really."

"Takes time," Mona replied, stroking Joey's hair.

"I know you're not talking about coffee," he said suddenly, almost defiantly.

Olivia's heart sank. Since the moment he'd been born she had wanted to protect him from harm, physical or emotional. She would never forget the first time her sunny child had his feelings hurt. Only three, he had tried to play with a few eight-year-olds. They rebuffed him, and his tiny face had crumpled in confusion. It was unreasonable, she knew. Obviously, she couldn't keep him from the inevitable pain and disappointments of life. But up until then nothing she had experienced had ever pained her more than that first incident.

And now the consequences were so much more. "No, sweetie, I'm not." She sank down on the edge of his bed. "When I disagree with Grandpa, it's my problem, not yours."

"About going away?" Although he tried to keep the defiance in his voice, a fearful note tinged the two words.

She reached out, pulling him into the kind of hug he no longer easily accepted or tolerated. "You're not going anywhere."

He lingered against her for a few moments, dropping his defenses. Jerking back suddenly, he scowled at her. "Why didn't you just say that?"

Feeling tears forming, she swallowed past the lump in her throat. "I should have. I keep forgetting how fast you're growing up."

The furrow remained between his eyebrows but his scowl diminished. "Why does Grandpa want to send me away?"

All the slights of her own childhood flashed in her thoughts, but she kept them to herself. "He doesn't. Grandpa thinks the army way is the only way to be happy. But I believe we have a lot more options."

"This is 'cause Dad's dead, huh?"

Olivia swallowed again. "Yes…and because you almost got expelled from school."

"But you got that fixed!" he protested.

Narrowing her eyes, she stared at him. "Got it fixed?"

For one sickening moment she wondered if her father was right, that she didn't have what it took to raise her son by herself.

"You know. Doing the work stuff so I can go back to school."

She searched his expression, wondering if he thought that she was a pushover, that he had gotten away with his crime.

Joey stood and went back to the terrarium to feed his turtle.

Her mother patted her shoulder.

Olivia clasped her hand for support. "Do you think I can always *fix it* when you get in trouble?"

Joey turned back around, frowning. And then she saw it, that flash of hurt he instantly hid. He no doubt thought she had little more faith in him than his grandfather. "Or have you decided it's better not to get in trouble?" she improvised, gentling her tone.

"Duh," he replied.

Sensing the hurt had been somewhat allayed, she ruffled his dark hair. "I've always known you were brilliant."

He rolled his eyes, then turned back to the terrarium.

Olivia met her mother's gaze. It had been a close escape. She didn't need any more of those. She would make sure of it. They would return to the community-service work and Zeke. But she didn't feel a sense of relief. Anticipation, anxiety and not a small measure of fear stirred her thoughts. She wasn't sure there was another close escape at hand.

Chapter Six

Zeke glanced out the large windows of the reception area as he checked over the day's appointments.

"She'll be here soon enough," Angie commented.

"Who?"

His tech grinned. "The tooth fairy." She resumed typing in the previous day's test results on her computer.

"You have something to say, spit it out."

"Me?" Eyebrows raised, Angie shook her head. "Nope."

Zeke turned on his heel and returned to his office. Determined to shake off her comment, he studied his list of expected patients. Not that the lineup was likely to stay the same. Emergencies, big and small, often intruded, shaking things up. Angie had a knack for fitting in animals that needed to be seen and determining if others could wait until the next day. But she was way off thinking he was watching for Olivia.

He thumped the list with a pen, looking up to make sure Angie wasn't lingering at his door, then looked out of his office window. Not that Olivia and Joey were late. Turned out after the one early breakfast they had shared, he'd woken up with the same urge every day since. But a week of pancakes didn't resolve the longing.

That one day in his kitchen had made the house seem like a home for the first time since he'd moved in. With Joey puttering and Olivia's hesitant but sweet smile… It was just breakfast.

Still…

He heard the heavy outside door open, then two sets of footsteps. He didn't need to look out the window again to know it was Olivia and Joey. Visualizing the knowing look on Angie's face if he popped out immediately, Zeke made himself wait. Hearing the murmur of three voices, he didn't move, listening to the timbre of their words. "Zeke?" Angie called out.

He glanced wryly at the seldom-used intercom button on his phone. It took only a few moments to cross his office to the reception area. "Yep."

"Need you to hand out assignments," Angie told him in an especially angelic voice.

He didn't need another matchmaker in his life. His parents had that role down pat.

"Have you had breakfast?" Zeke asked them.

Joey fiddled with the stack of folders on Angie's desk. "Yeah. It wasn't as good as your pancakes."

Olivia widened her eyes at Zeke as she nodded unobtrusively toward her son.

Point taken. But Zeke was surprised Joey was still thinking about that one breakfast. "Every day can't be pancake day." Zeke met Olivia's eyes in silent apology. "Coffee?"

She hesitated only a moment. "Sounds good."

Angie rose. "I'd better make a fresh pot. It's down to the dregs."

Waving her hands, Olivia protested. "I can do it. I'm here to help, not make more work for you, Angie."

"Actually, I was headed in there anyway." Zeke spoke

up. "Angie's right. I make the first pot strong enough to remove paint."

"But—"

Ignoring her protest, Zeke headed toward the kitchen, trailed by a reluctant Olivia.

"Really," she insisted, "I think I can make a pot of coffee."

"And I know where we keep the coffee and filters."

She followed him into the kitchen. "Okay. Then I need to learn where things are. This probably won't be the only pot of coffee I make." So far she had only walked dogs, helped restock supplies and swept. Every time she stopped for a break, Angie had fresh coffee and usually a treat ready.

He paused, wondering. Did she plan to keep coming with Joey? He had been surprised when she put in a full week.

"Every time we moved," she reminisced, "things got put in a new place, so I'm used to hunting for what I need." She met his eyes. "The houses were always so different."

"You didn't live in base housing?"

"Post housing. The army has forts, not bases." Olivia looked nostalgic. "And it depended on the fort, what was available. I didn't know that when I was little, just that I never could guess where we'd be living next. Military housing's better for officers but my dad went at it the hard way. Joined as enlisted, went to college, then OTC—officer's training." She smiled ruefully. "My mother was determined to make each place home. I learned how to paint walls before I could write. And we always had the most colorful house on the block—Mom wanted to be a decorator and our houses were her only canvases. Money was tight and most of the wives made army causes their causes. But she was different. *We* were different." Olivia paused, then flushed. "Sorry, I didn't mean to bore you with all that."

"You didn't." He plopped the can of coffee on the counter. "And you'll find plenty of nomads almost everywhere."

Her smile was wry but sad. "I suppose so."

Reaching up, he grabbed a new pack of coffee filters and automatically put them on a lower shelf that Angie could reach. Olivia was a few inches taller than his assistant. He smiled, thinking Olivia would find a way to climb to the top of the tall old cabinets if she had to. Part bulldog, this woman.

"What?" she asked.

"Just glad we had a spare pack of filters," he improvised, thinking she might not like his canine comparison. "Just a standard drip coffeepot, nothing fancy."

"I do miss the coffee shops in Austin. A caramel macchiato is hard to beat."

"My sister has one of those fancy machines that makes all kinds of coffee drinks."

Surprised, she tilted her head. "You're right—I could make my own."

"Angie says I should call the coffee I make espresso, it's so strong." He shrugged. "It suits me."

Her eyes drifted up toward his. "I suppose it does."

Violet, he thought suddenly. Her eyes reminded him of some exotic jewel. In a way, Olivia herself gave him that impression. She wasn't like anyone he'd known before. She was…different. Hard on herself, softer than she realized on others.

His hand grazed the coffee filters and he returned to earth. "Coffee won't make itself." He gave her a quick demonstration of the coffeepot, realizing he was talking to cover the reaction she'd caused. "Doesn't take long to brew."

"Do you want me to bring you a cup?" she asked, seeming unaware of the effect of her gaze.

"Um…no," he said, fumbling. "My mug's in the other room." He looked at his watch, scarcely registering the time. "But I'd better get to work."

"Oh, what about our assignments?"

At the moment he couldn't have assigned a monkey to eat a banana. "Let me look over the schedule." Once he'd retreated back to his office, Zeke finally allowed a whooshing sigh. He hadn't gotten that wound up over a woman in who knew how long.

Olivia absently tapped slim fingers on the counter. If she'd caused Zeke that much discomfort just making coffee, this was going to be a long project. Not that she was terribly surprised. It seemed that she was always a step behind everyone else. Olivia had often wondered if it would have been the same had she grown up in just one place. Would she have belonged then? Or was it just her?

Zeke couldn't have any preconceptions—they had just met a week ago. Yet she sensed his unease. He had practically fled from the kitchen. Maybe it was time to accept it once and for all. She *was* different. She never caught on to inside jokes, references, insinuations. Suddenly she was eight years old again, trying to play with the girls in her new neighborhood.

There had been giggles and whispers. Brittany, the leader of the group, had told her that she couldn't play with them because she wasn't one of them—girls who had been friends since birth.

Olivia absently replaced the can of coffee and pack of filters, scanning the cabinets for mugs. Funny—she hadn't felt quite as out of place in the veterinary clinic as she'd thought she would. But Zeke had just demonstrated how uncomfortable he was around her. Not a good sign.

Angie was friendly, welcoming. That was all she really needed, Olivia told herself. So what if the handsome doctor wasn't comfortable around her? She'd known worse. Yet her gaze strayed to the back of the kitchen and the doorway leading to the other side of the building, where he was working.

By the time the coffee finished brewing, Olivia had found a mug for herself. Remembering that Angie was drinking green tea these days, Olivia carried the mugs back into the reception room.

"You didn't have to do that!" Angie exclaimed, reaching for her mug. "But I confess I was too tired to get up." She patted her stomach.

Olivia felt a pang of unexpected jealousy. She had always wanted one more child, but Ted had wanted to wait. Pushing the envy aside, Olivia smiled softly. "How far along are you?"

"Four months." Angie looked down ruefully at her mounded tummy. "We've been trying a long time. This baby is the answer to many, many prayers."

Totally unprepared for the spurt of tears Angie's words caused, Olivia forced them away. "That's wonderful."

Angie chuckled. "My husband, Gary, treats me like breakable china and it's pretty sweet."

"Sounds like a nice guy."

Angie's face was all happiness. "Wants me to stop working—actually, he's been on me about that since the day we found out. But I can't desert Zeke."

"You'll need time after the baby's born."

Angie sighed. "I know and it worries me. But this isn't

like the city, with a zillion qualified vet techs. Plus, I do the books and office stuff, too."

"Chief cook and bottle washer, as my dad would say."

"Exactly. And I like to think my work matters."

"Clearly it does!" Olivia sank down into the chair angled beside the desk. "I haven't been around long but it seems like you're the doctor's right arm and leg."

Nodding, Angie accepted the compliment. "I love my work, but we've waited a long time for this baby, and family comes first."

"Of course."

"Which leaves Zeke without a tech and office manager."

Olivia frowned. "Have you put out any feelers to see if someone in the area is qualified?"

"I've talked to every vet's office within a hundred miles. Found out there's a shortage of vet techs."

"Which doesn't leave you any closer to a solution." Olivia cocked her head. "Maybe someone in Austin who's looking to move to a rural area?"

"I have ads out on the internet, but no one's turned up yet." She patted her stomach again. "I've prayed about it and I know it'll turn out all right."

Olivia didn't have a reply for that. God had proven He wasn't watching over Ted. How could she believe He would watch over anyone else?

"I didn't mean to be such a downer," Angie proclaimed. "Should have said what I meant to begin with. This is sweet of you to bring me tea."

"It's nothing. You work hard and…" Olivia shrugged.

"Thank you. I always considered myself lucky working with Zeke because he's so considerate. Nice to have another woman around who is, as well."

Olivia felt herself flush.

"I think we have five minutes to spare." Angie opened

a drawer and pulled out a box of shortbread cookies, offering them to Olivia. "Have you seen the new shipment over at Barton's Shoes?"

Olivia shook her head.

"Now, that's something you absolutely can't miss."

Having collected himself, Zeke walked with Joey to the barn. "We've got some stalls that have to be mucked out."

"Is 'mucked' what I think it is?"

Zeke glanced down into the boy's intelligent eyes. "Yep. It's part of owning animals or doctoring them. We don't have a lot of overnight domestic stock, but my horses and Milkdud have to be taken care of every day."

Joey looked puzzled. "Who does it when there's no community-service worker?"

"Me."

"But you're the doctor."

"And animal owner. If you care about your animals, then you do the chores that come along with ownership. Sure, there are big ranchers and breeders who have fulltime help. But me? Nope."

Joey frowned. "How come you don't just hire somebody?"

"When I'm grooming my horses, I have time to think, clear my head. No phones, television, internet. Just quiet."

"But you said you always have your beeper."

Zeke's grin was rueful. "That comes with being a vet. I like my quiet time, but I can't miss an emergency call. Folks around here don't call me at night unless it's important."

"Oh."

"I know you haven't lived in Rosewood long, but I'm guessing you've seen it's different than the city. Everybody knows everybody else. And being a considerate neighbor means a lot."

Joey shrugged.

He thought of the trouble Joey had gotten into at school. Zeke didn't automatically accept every community-service worker. It depended on what they'd done. He didn't judge, but he was responsible for the safety of the animals placed in his care. "Do you think back in the city you'd have gotten community service instead of being expelled?"

Joey's face paled. "I dunno."

Zeke was fairly certain he did. "Point is, we treat people the way we want to be treated."

"Isn't that the Golden Rule?"

"It's a rule to live by. If you wouldn't want someone to steal from you, you shouldn't steal from anyone else."

Joey flushed deeply. "So my mom told you."

"Nope."

Suspicious, Joey looked at him.

"I always check out the people I'm going to work with. I talked to the principal."

Joey flinched.

"And the school secretary. She told me what a good kid you are."

Staring at him in disbelief, Joey stepped backward.

"A few bad decisions don't make you a bad person. It's what you do about them that determines who you'll be."

"Mucking out the barn's gonna do that?"

Zeke grinned. "If it did, I could charge a hundred dollars an hour for psychotherapy."

Their coffee break over, Angie showed Olivia the relatively simple filing system. "I have to admit, I leave filing for the end of the day. Rather do just about anything else."

"I don't mind." Olivia slipped a paper into a folder. "It's orderly, just like I was brought up."

Angie chuckled as the phone rang. "Harrison's." She listened quietly.

Olivia heard a few "ums" and "ohs." Sensing the call was personal, she concentrated on the filing, trying not to listen.

However, she couldn't ignore the huge sigh Angie emitted when she hung up the phone.

"Is everything okay?"

Angie frowned. "Not really. That was my doctor's office. Based on my latest test results, they want me to have more bed rest than I'm getting now."

"Full-time?"

"Not yet." Angie scanned the office. "Not that it matters. This is full-time, not part-time."

Olivia spoke quickly before she could change her mind. "What if I did the office work? So your hours would only be for the tech work? You could get the bed rest you need."

Angie looked stunned and relieved. "I don't know...."

"I learn quickly," Olivia encouraged. "I've done billing work and filing, answered phones."

"But this is just a temporary thing for you and for Joey."

"Doesn't have to be." Olivia clutched the pile of papers yet to be filed. "They rarely need me at the drugstore. I have lots of empty days. In fact, they wouldn't miss me if I left."

Understanding filled Angie's eyes. "If Zeke's okay with it, I guess we could give it a try."

Relief, peppered with a touch of excitement, filled her. Olivia brushed away any reasoning that said she was playing with something that she might not be able to control.

Chapter Seven

Olivia sat at the reception desk updating the week's medical charts and entering procedures and charges according to Angie's or Zeke's notes. She was still learning the computer program. Good thing Angie wasn't far away. Just in the back processing new blood samples if she had any questions.

It was daunting to man the front desk for the first time. She half expected someone to rush in with a bloodied animal. And what would she do? Handle the situation calmly or completely freak out? So far the scariest task had been deciding whether it was appropriate to sort the mail.

Hearing the door open, Olivia looked up. A short, six-tyish woman with curly silver-threaded red hair smiled widely as she walked in. Stopping in front of the desk, she cocked her head. "I don't believe I know you."

"I…" Olivia cleared her throat. "I'm filling in for Angie while she's doing her tech work."

The woman's smile widened ever farther. "I'm Nancy Harrison, Zeke's mother."

Olivia automatically straightened her already-straight back. "Hello." She struggled for a reply. "Um…do you want me to beep him?"

Nancy shook her head. "I didn't get your name."

Olivia flushed and smiled. "Olivia Gray."

"It's about time Zeke got some more help around here. Angie's a workhorse—excuse the pun—but after the baby comes…" Nancy nodded in a knowing mother's way.

"Well, Zeke didn't hire me—"

Nancy's sudden frown was as staunch as her inviting smile had been. "You're on probation?"

Swallowing, Olivia explained about Joey's crime and community-service sentence.

Puzzlement replaced the frown on Nancy's face. "That doesn't exactly explain why *you're* here."

"Oh, that. I offered."

"Don't blame you. I'd want to be able to keep an eye on my boy, too. Especially since he's only twelve. Not everyone's as fair as Zeke."

Olivia immediately liked Nancy's assumption that Zeke couldn't be anything except fair. "True."

Nancy's bright blue eyes sparkled with curiosity. "So what do you think?"

Olivia blinked, not certain if Mrs. Harrison was referring to the veterinary practice or Zeke. "I'm not sure…"

Waving her arms, Nancy gestured toward the exam area and Zeke's office.

"It's interesting," Olivia replied, relieved she meant the practice.

Nancy chuckled. "Needn't pussyfoot with me. I know the veterinary business can be exhausting and sometimes heartbreaking. Oh, sure, it's fulfilling, too." She eyed the stack of notes. "But I'm not sure everything's *interesting*."

"Busted," Olivia admitted with a smile. "I've been learning this program all week and it's a challenge. But working here's much more interesting than my part-time job at the drugstore was. I gave that up since it was only a few hours a week and they didn't really need me."

"And so you can be home for your husband?"

Olivia shook her head. "I'm a widow." She couldn't bring herself to use the term *passed on.* It whitewashed what had really happened.

Nancy's entire face softened in sympathy. "I'm so sorry, my dear. Raising a young son alone is a full-time job in itself." She sank into the chair beside the desk, and her now-gentle eyes searched Olivia's face. "And that leaves no one to care for you."

"Well, I'm an adult—"

"And a woman. Don't misunderstand me. I don't think every woman must have a man. But we all need care, sometimes a lot of care."

It was something Olivia missed fiercely. She nodded, afraid her voice would warble.

Leaning forward, Nancy patted her hand. "I've upset you. It's this silly mouth of mine. I just open it and everything I'm thinking spills out. No filter."

Olivia wasn't one to make sudden decisions, but she instantly liked Zeke's mother. "It's good to talk about it sometimes, too."

Reflecting, Nancy agreed. "That's why we need our girlfriends. Sometimes only another woman understands. I hope you have good ones."

Silent, Olivia was at a loss for words. She didn't know if she could yet count Kate as a friend, even though she felt a strong kinship.

Nancy's brow furrowed. "I haven't seen you around town before. Are you new to Rosewood?"

"We've only lived here about a year and a half."

"Then it's high time you come to a Harrison Sunday meal. We head over to the house right after church. My girls help me put lunch together while my boys filch whatever they can until it's ready."

"Oh, you don't have to—"

"I *want* you to come. You and your son. I have grandchildren close to his age and all the way down to toddlers."

Intrigued, Olivia forgot her reserve. "Sounds like a big family."

"Zeke made it a perfect half dozen. Three daughters, three sons. Now most of them are providing another generation for me to enjoy." Nancy shook her head. "Except for Zeke. Never married."

"I'm sure when it's time, he'll find the right woman."

Nancy's expression turned speculative. "Timing. Yes, that's all important. Speaking of which, I have to be back in town in about ten minutes. I have an appointment with Beth to get something done to this mop of hair."

"I think it's pretty."

Laughing, Nancy patted her hand again. "You are sweet. I'll plan to see you Sunday after church."

Olivia hesitated, then admitted the truth to Mrs. Harrison. "I don't go to church."

"We all have our own ways to worship," Nancy replied, seemingly unperturbed. "Now, I'd better scoot."

Realizing she had occupied all of Nancy's time, Olivia grabbed a pen. "Do you want to leave a message for Zeke?"

Eyes sparkling, Nancy declined. "I'll catch up with him later." She reached for a pen and scribbled her address on a notepad. "See you Sunday."

Watching her leave, Olivia shook her head, amazed that Mrs. Harrison had maneuvered her into attending the first social occasion outside of dinner with her own parents since Ted's death. And she'd managed it in under fifteen minutes. What had Nancy said about timing? Whatever it was, the woman was an expert. Now all Olivia had to do was face Zeke's entire family.

By Sunday, Olivia's nerves were beyond shredded. They were minced, mangled and mushed. Joey had taken the lunch invitation in stride. But she had been on edge since Friday, waiting for Zeke to say something. But the afternoon had passed without a comment. Saturday had, as well.

Having tried on and rejected five outfits, Olivia sank to the edge of her bed. She had no clue what to expect. Would the rest of the family be as warm and friendly as Nancy? Or were they more formal and reserved? She rejected a stark black wool dress. Finally settling on a butter-yellow dress made of cool cotton, Olivia checked the mirror for at least the dozenth time.

Feeling as she had all her life when confronted with new people, Olivia felt her stomach knot. She wasn't a schoolgirl anymore, she reminded herself. But gazing in the mirror, butterflies flew loops in her stomach.

"Mom?" Joey called out.

"In here." She made a half turn when he appeared at the doorway. "How do I look?"

Joey shrugged.

There was still plenty of rough road to cover in their relationship. She loved him so much she wanted to hug him until he hollered. Instead Olivia smiled and glanced at his clothes. "Well, you look good. Nice choice."

Joey tugged at his blue dress shirt. "Still don't get why I can't just wear a T-shirt and jeans."

"Because this isn't a T-shirt-and-jeans kind of lunch." The others would all be coming from church, but Olivia didn't want to remind him of the fact that they no longer attended church. He had been so wounded after Ted's death that he hadn't questioned the change. She hoped there wouldn't be too many questions on the subject from Zeke's family.

Zeke's family. She strove to maintain her cheerful expression, but her knees wobbled at the thought. It wasn't only that she worried she wouldn't fit in. What would Zeke make of them being there?

"Are we going or what?" Joey asked.

She swallowed and headed toward the front door.

The drive was far, far too short. Located in one of the oldest neighborhoods in Rosewood, the brick street was wide enough for the wagons that had traveled it back in the 1800s.

Several cars were parked out front and in the driveway of the two-story Victorian house. Still, it was easy to find a spot to park. Turning off the ignition, Olivia stared at the lovely old house. But she wasn't thinking about the manicured flower beds or the tall, graceful trees. No…

"Mom!" Joey said in an exasperated tone.

"Right. Well, we're here."

Wishing her stomach would stop knotting, Olivia stepped out of their car, acting as though it were just any other occasion. One that didn't make her palms sweat and her throat dry up.

Joey stared up at the top of the house. "They got a porch up on the roof."

Tilting her head back, Olivia saw the Victorian widow's walk he referred to.

The door swung open and Nancy popped outside. "I thought I spotted you!" She smiled at Joey. "And you must be Joey. I'm Nancy Harrison, Zeke's mother."

Joey ducked his head.

Nancy draped an arm around his shoulder. "My grandchildren can't wait to meet you."

A string of names flashed by as Nancy introduced each son and daughter, their spouses and children. Olivia smiled at each in turn, promptly forgetting every single name. Except one. Zeke.

He had welcomed her, then swept Joey off to mingle with the other kids.

Nancy Harrison stayed by her side as people drifted around the yard. "I forget sometimes that we're a little overwhelming to people who haven't met us, especially when everyone's here."

"I think it's wonderful...your big family, I mean."

Erica, Zeke's oldest sister, had lingered, as well. "I suppose I wouldn't trade any of them now, but fifteen years ago..." She laughed. "Little brothers are awful when you're first trying to date."

"They were kind of horrible about that," Nancy admitted cheerfully.

"Do you have siblings?" Erica questioned.

Olivia shook her head. "Just me. Now just Joey."

"He seems like a great kid." Erica pointed over to the swing set. "Look how good he's being with Melanie's little monsters. Did you say he's twelve?"

"Yes."

"Most twelve-year-olds won't bother with younger kids."

Watching, Olivia warmed to the sight of her son carefully pushing swings for the little ones.

Nancy linked her arm with Olivia's. "I was an only child and always wanted lots of brothers and sisters."

"So she inflicted them on us," Erica added lightheartedly.

"Didn't keep you from having your own kids," Nancy retorted mildly.

"How old are your children?" Olivia questioned, not

used to being treated as though she'd known the family forever.

"Lilly is nine and Cade is eleven. My son will be here in a few minutes with his dad. They stopped at the house to pick up a soccer ball. Mom and Dad usually have every kind of sports ball, but the soccer ball got killed when the big boys were playing with it."

Olivia chuckled, imagining Zeke and his brothers in a game.

Nancy laughed, as well. "Did my heart good. They may be adults, but they'll always be my little boys."

Erica rolled her eyes. "See what I have to deal with?"

Shyly, Olivia smiled.

"Being the oldest has always been quite the burden for Erica," Nancy teased, looking affectionately at her daughter.

"Mom probably thinks of it more as the experiment child," Erica explained. "If it didn't kill Erica, it probably won't hurt the others."

Laughing, Nancy shook her head. "You know how it is, Olivia. Children don't come with instruction manuals. And I couldn't help being extra careful with Erica."

"I was the only child in preschool with my name, address and phone number sewn onto the front of my shirt," Erica said. "And since we live in this wild and scary town, nobody even skipped a beat." Again Erica rolled her eyes.

Olivia smiled. "I did sew an ID label inside Joey's T-shirt."

"Inside, yes. In large letters on the front? Not so much. But it paved the way for Ken and Del. Even Melanie. By the time they had Heidi, she got away with murder."

Funny—Olivia noticed she hadn't mentioned Zeke. Then again, there were a lot of Harrisons.

"She's exaggerating," Nancy protested. "The older ones looked out a lot for the younger ones."

Erica waved at a tall man and a boy who looked about Joey's age. "Well, that's my missing duo. Olivia, I'll give you a break and bring them over in a few minutes. I'm guessing you've already forgotten everyone's names."

Olivia exhaled as Erica left. It wasn't as though meeting new people were something she hadn't done. She had literally spent her life in this kind of situation, but it was thoughtful of Erica to notice.

"She's really nice."

"I think they're pretty much all keepers," Nancy admitted fondly. "I do hope I didn't ambush you with everyone at once."

"Please don't give it a second thought. I've been doing it all my life—meeting new people, I mean."

"Really?"

"I'm an army brat. It goes with the territory."

Nancy's wide grin softened to concern. "That must have been hard."

Olivia shrugged. "Just the way it was."

"I didn't invite quite as many people today," Nancy said. "Sometimes the house and yard are overflowing. We have a few regulars who always come and they've pretty much become family over the years."

Olivia blanched. "I hope it's not because of us."

"Only in a good way. Zeke told me that you haven't lived in Rosewood all that long. Thought maybe you'd like to meet a few people your own age. And I have to confess, it's nice sometimes to have a smaller group like this."

Olivia looked around the yard. It was full of people.

"I hope you'll come to feel at home here in Rosewood." Nancy's voice gentled even more. "You're so young to have lost your husband. I won't say that I know how you feel, because I can't even imagine that much pain." Her blue eyes filled with empathy. "I hope you'll come to consider us family, too. No one can ever have too much family, and we always have room for more." Her voice dipped for a moment, a husky note taking over. "Zeke tells me your parents live in Rosewood, too, so I know you don't need a second set, but brothers and sisters, they don't have to be by birth."

Nancy glanced up and her smile widened as she waved. "Here's someone you'll really like."

Olivia followed her gaze and spotted Kate with a tall, handsome man and a pretty teenager. "I've already met Kate, but not her family."

"Even better."

When Kate and her family reached them, Olivia smiled. "A familiar face."

"Nancy, I'm guessing you taught your kids how to swim by throwing them in the water," Kate exclaimed. "Olivia, are you surviving this mob?"

"Very nicely."

"This is my husband, Tucker."

Very tall and handsome, Kate's husband held out his hand. "Feel like I know you already. Kate's been talking about you nonstop."

Flushing, Olivia couldn't imagine what she'd been saying.

"And this is our beautiful daughter, Alyssa," Kate added.

Alyssa looked sufficiently embarrassed by the introduction. "Hi. Mom always says stuff like that."

"Because it's true," Tucker told her. "Come on, squirt, let's check out what's on the grill."

Kate seemed content to let them stroll away. "So glad

Nancy invited you. I stopped by your house a couple times this week but didn't catch you at home."

"Oh, I've been working at the clinic—in the office." Olivia explained Angie's condition and how they were sharing the job.

"Hope that's enough," Kate said after a moment. "She's waited a long time for this baby. So you stepped up and offered to help?"

"Sure did," Nancy replied for her. "You'd think she'd known us her whole life. She didn't hesitate, even told Angie that she and Joey would do all the pet exercising."

Olivia blushed. "Really, it's not that big of a deal."

Nancy lifted her eyebrows. "Don't believe it. You know Angie's always been Zeke's right arm. And it's not as though he's got a wife or girlfriend who could help him."

Kate shot Olivia an encouraging look.

Surely Nancy wasn't playing matchmaker?

Clearing her throat, the woman in question waved toward the long table that was steadily filling with bowls and casserole dishes. "Guess I'd better check on things."

"Can I help?" Olivia asked.

"No, enjoy your time with Kate. Glad she's a familiar face."

"So…" they began simultaneously as Nancy walked away.

Laughter erupted.

"How is it I feel as though I've known you for years instead of weeks?" Olivia asked when her breath returned.

Kate shook her head. "Because you're different."

"Different?" Olivia's voice faltered.

"Like me. I know that Tucker is the one who was widowed, but it's like we share that bond. You know what I mean?"

She did. "Hadn't thought of why, just that I'm not nervous or tense around you."

Kate didn't question her response, only nodding. "There's something about Rosewood. People accepting each other for who they are. I'm not a native, but I feel like I am. Never thought I'd leave Houston. Certainly not for a small town. But I really don't miss anything."

"I don't miss the city itself, just the variety of stores and restaurants. I was telling Zeke that mostly I miss my daily caramel macchiato," Olivia confessed. "I used to grab one after I'd dropped Joey off at school. Not exactly an earth-shattering loss."

"Hmm. Have you thought about buying one of those fancy coffee machines? Or we could talk to Maddie, who owns the Tea Cart. She's always open to new ideas. I haven't been there for a while, so I don't remember everything that's on the menu." Kate tilted her head. "Tea is her main thing, but she serves coffee, too. I don't know about drinks like caramel macchiatos. I hadn't thought about it, but I always loved my lattes when I lived in the city. I'm used to Tucker's coffee that's strong enough to make your stomach turn cartwheels. Sure wakes me up, though."

"I've never been to the Tea Cart." Or many places in Rosewood, Kate realized.

"You've missed out. I'm guessing you get some sort of lunch break. Let's plan on going this week."

"Okay." Two invitations in one week. Olivia grinned, unguarded laughter spilling out. She was practically becoming a social butterfly. "Now, fill me in on how it's going interviewing my dad for the portrait."

Zeke watched Olivia with fascination. He had never seen her laugh like that or seem so relaxed, so natural.

She'd always been so stiff and unbending, so much so she almost defined the word *rigid*.

At least when she knew anyone was looking. He continued to stare. Or was it only when she knew he was looking?

"Your eyeballs are practically on the ground now," Erica remarked, startling him.

"You came out of nowhere," he replied, rattled.

She held up two bottles of root beer. "Want one?"

"Yeah. Sure."

"There's a lot to that one," she commented, handing him the second bottle. "And if you say 'Which one?' I'll remind you why I'm the noogie queen."

"Olivia looks so different."

Erica glanced across the yard. "Happy, you mean?"

"Guess so. She's always so uptight at the clinic."

"Maybe she's uptight around people she doesn't know very well."

He shrugged. "It's been a while now."

"Oh, excuse me. Didn't know it was a relationship of practically decades."

"Not decades. I mean a relationship. Not a relationship." He calmed the words rushing to get out. "You know what I mean."

"But do you?"

He stared down at his sister. "What's that's supposed to mean?"

"I haven't seen anyone look so moon-eyed since Melanie met Jim."

"Olivia's just helping out at my clinic. She won't even let me put her on the payroll."

Erica lifted one shoulder. "You can pretend to be dense with the guys, but I know different."

Exhaling, Zeke absently wiped the condensation from

his bottle. "Look, Erica. I barely know the woman. She's a widow. Not somebody I'm going to ask out."

"Because she wouldn't want to just date casually? She'd expect a real relationship?"

"You ought to get that degree in psychiatry framed."

"Someone's getting testy."

"Erica, you're blessed. Great husband and kids. That doesn't mean you have to always play matchmaker. Mom and Dad are bad enough."

"Oh, little brother. Do you think we aren't all going to keep trying until it works?"

"Don't you have anybody else to bug today?"

Erica took a sip from the cold soda. "Sure. But no one as much fun as you."

Erica had always riled him up, teased him, practically made him stand on his head, but deep down she always had his back, had fought as much *for* him as *with* him. And that made her scarier than a mad bull at ten paces.

The afternoon dawdled by at times and whooshed by at others. Olivia and Kate had barely talked when lunch began. All of Zeke's siblings made a point to spend some time with her, and each one was as welcoming as their mother. Zeke's dad, who had been manning the grill, sat beside her for some time. She couldn't really remember what they'd talked about, just that it had been easy, companionable. Funny—she couldn't remember ever feeling that way around her own father. Immediately, she felt guilty for the thought.

Before she could dwell on it, games began. Nets were set up on both sides of the large yard. It was all informal, noisy and cozy.

"So this is what a big family's like," she murmured to Zeke as he handed her a badminton racket.

"You should have seen the lines to the bathroom when we were growing up. Blink and you lost your turn."

She shrugged. "Minor inconveniences."

"And dishes. Do you have any idea how many dishes we went through in a day? We all had to take turns doing everything."

"It's probably why you're so self-sufficient," she replied, thinking how orderly his house and practice were.

"I think that was the point."

"Do you wish you'd had a smaller family?" Olivia questioned.

"Never. Even when they drive me crazy. But it was a lot of work for my parents."

"They don't seem to mind," she ventured.

"I don't think Dad knew what he was getting into when my mother said she wanted a big family." He laughed. "It's a wonder they aren't bonkers." Reflection deepened his voice. "They're the best."

"I really like them," Olivia confided, realizing she'd been more open in this one day than in years.

"They like you," he replied.

She wondered at his tone. "That didn't sound genuine."

"It was. They genuinely like you."

She didn't see any pleasure in his expression. She was silent for a moment. Then she asked, "Do you not want them to like me?"

"Why would I want that?" Zeke picked up a plastic badminton birdie, resting it on his racket.

"I don't know." Olivia frowned. "But you sound like that's exactly what you want."

Zeke sighed. "My sister's been nagging me today. I didn't mean to take it out on you."

Not sure whether to believe him, she didn't respond.

"For as long as I can remember," Zeke continued, "Erica's been able to get under my skin like nobody else."

"Is it serious?"

"No, nothing like that. Guess we just know each other too well."

Baffled, Olivia didn't know what to say.

Zeke bounced the birdie on his racket again. "So we going to play?"

"I guess."

He handed her the birdie. "Ladies serve first."

"I haven't played since high school," she admitted.

"Then we should be perfectly matched."

The words hung in the air, then filtered through the lattice of late-spring leaves. She locked eyes with Zeke. And imagined the thought.

Chapter Eight

A volleyball smacked Zeke hard enough to nearly knock him off his feet. "Hey, keep to your side of the yard," he yelled, pelting the ball back hard enough to thwack the fence when his brother Ken ducked. "Idiots," he muttered.

"I'm sure it wasn't on purpose," Olivia suggested.

Zeke shook his head. "You don't know my brothers."

Her expression turned tentative again.

Feeling responsible, he forced himself to relax. "Ken and Del would think I was sick if I let it go."

Still looking perplexed, Olivia shrugged. "Must be a sibling thing I don't understand."

It was something she wouldn't understand, all right. Like how he must be practically mooning over her like a teenager. If Erica had noticed…

Olivia smiled hopefully. "Ready to play?"

"Sure."

In the Harrison family, Zeke was the Terminator when it came to badminton. Even his oldest brother, Ken, who usually ruled in football and soccer, rarely won.

The birdie passed by his racket again and Zeke made himself stop staring at his opponent. As he pivoted to fetch the errant shuttlecock, he reminded himself Olivia was a widow. Hands off.

She shook her honey-colored hair back and he noticed how the sunlight picked up random strands of blond and auburn. It went well with her ivory skin and those amazing eyes. Realizing he was all but gaping at her, Zeke tossed the birdie over the net. "Your serve."

Olivia smiled, not the way his siblings would have if he'd missed such an easy return. Instead she toned down her serve.

And for some reason, Zeke couldn't make himself smash the return.

It seemed strange that all that was familiar—his family, their chatter and laughter, his friends, the yard itself—faded away. And in the foreground was Olivia. Only Olivia.

She laughed as she bent to scoop up the birdie that had flown by. "Seems more like I played this last when I was in elementary instead of high school! How many misses so far?"

He ignored all the little voices that buzzed through his head. "Not really counting. We're playing a friendly game."

Olivia tossed the shuttlecock over the net. "Then I'd hate to be up against you if you were bent on winning!"

He'd always been bent on winning. When he had been the toughest kid in every foster home, when he had come to live with his parents and was determined not to be loved, when he had gone to college, when he had wooed Belinda. But something about Olivia pushed those victories and defeats further back than he had been able to in the past.

She had kicked off her shoes. And in her winsome yellow dress, Olivia looked young enough to be a college girl.

He wondered if she had smiled more then, before she'd lost her husband.

Olivia patted her racket. "Ready when you are!"

Barely focused, he served. She made the return and he stepped up his game, liking it when she raced up to the net for short returns and when she ran long, her slim calves flashing by.

"Whew!" she said breathlessly after picking up a missed birdie. "Can we go back to being friendly?"

Zeke doubted it. Somehow, the barrier in his mind that had been locked against a relationship slipped. And he doubted it could be rebuilt.

Hardly able to believe she had stayed until evening, Olivia thanked Nancy for the lovely day.

"Then I expect you back," Nancy told her. "You and Joey."

Joey was reluctantly giving up his game of soccer even though it was too dark to play.

"My kids would mash me if I turned on the backyard lights," Nancy explained. "Since tomorrow's a school day."

"I've really enjoyed myself," Olivia repeated, making sure Mrs. Harrison knew how much she had appreciated the day.

Nancy reached out with a warm hug. "And we enjoyed having you. Promise me you'll come next Sunday."

Olivia looked toward Zeke, who stood not too far away. "I don't want to be a nuisance."

"As though you ever could be." Nancy's bright blue eyes were soft in the dusky evening. "It has been our pleasure meeting you today."

Flushing, Olivia gazed down.

"I'll take that as a yes."

Olivia jerked her head up, trying to see Zeke's reaction. But his back was turned to her.

Nancy squeezed her hand. "Pretty soon you'll wonder what you did on Sunday afternoons before you became part of us."

Part of us. Magical words. Unfamiliar words. Inviting, lovely words.

Then Zeke turned back to them. "Come on, Joey." He rounded up the straggler.

"Looks like you're ready, Olivia," he continued.

"Yes, just saying goodbye to your mother."

"I'll drive you home."

Puzzled, she scrunched her eyebrows together. "I drove here."

"I know. Saw your car. But I'll take you and Joey home."

"But your truck is here."

"And it's dark. I'll drive you home."

"Surely you're not concerned about our safety in Rosewood?"

"A lady doesn't go home alone at night." Zeke's tone was unyielding as he took the lead toward her car.

Pulling her keys from her purse, she waved them in the air. "But how are you going to get back?"

"Walk."

"There's really no need…"

Zeke plucked the keys from her hand. "Joey, you ready?"

"Yeah."

Not quite sure what she was feeling, Olivia allowed him to take control as they got into her car. "I appreciate your concern, but you don't have to put yourself out."

Zeke glanced over at her. "I could use the air walking back."

"You were out in the backyard practically all day!"

"Not all of the day. Maybe next week you'll join us at church in the morning."

The unexpected invitation hit her like a sledgehammer. Uncomfortably aware of Joey in the backseat, she tightened her lips. "Thank you, but no."

This time Zeke's gaze lingered. "A story for another time?"

Her eyes implored him to stop asking.

Thankfully, he did. Exhaling, she grasped the handle of her purse, anxious to be home.

But once they arrived, she was at a loss again. Did she just thank him and send him on his way? "Zeke, would you like a cup of coffee?"

"Decaf?"

She managed a smile. "Read my mind."

Trying to seem nonchalant, she fished in her purse for the keys, then remembered he had them.

"You keep the doors locked?" Zeke asked, passing her the keys.

"Well, yes."

"Probably used to it from living in the city. Don't really need to do that here."

Olivia thought of all the nights she'd lain alone in bed thinking of how vulnerable she and Joey were. No man of the house to make her feel safe. Despite her dad's deployments, she hadn't been frightened when they lived in military housing. Feeling the security of the army surrounding them had been comforting. And those times when they didn't live in military housing, her mother had seemed so sure, so secure, leaving no room for fear.

She pushed open the door and turned the living-room light on. She hadn't expected to be gone so long. Otherwise Zeke would have noticed the telltale light she kept on in the evenings.

Joey headed toward his room.

"Do you want some milk?" Olivia asked before he disappeared.

"Nah."

"Wasn't that long ago that he would have hung out with me watching TV," she reminisced.

"Probably needs some time alone after the crowd today," Zeke replied. "He's at that age—not a little boy, yet not a young man."

"I suppose it's wrong of me to wish he could stay a little boy forever."

"Not wrong, just impossible."

Hearing the understanding in his voice, she relaxed a fraction. "I'll put that coffee on."

Zeke wandered toward the bookcase. "Do you want some help?"

"No. I'm good." She was glad of the time alone to take stock of the fact that a man stood in her living room. Absently she rubbed the empty spot on her ring finger. When she had worn her wedding band, people had asked about Ted. She found it too difficult to keep repeating what had happened, so after six months she had tucked the band into her jewelry box. Now she wondered what signal it sent to leave that finger bare.

Olivia grabbed two mugs and poured a little cream into hers. She knew Zeke took his black.

It took only a few minutes to brew the small pot of coffee. On impulse, Olivia put a few brownies on a plate, as well.

Zeke glanced up when she returned to the living room. "You don't have to serve me."

"It's all right. I don't have that much company, so it's really no bother." She put the small wooden tray on the coffee table. "I made brownies this morning. I thought you'd like some."

He reached for one. "I'll never say no to brownies."

"Joey likes them. Luckily, he goes through them fast enough that I don't eat too many."

Zeke's appraisal was easy, almost undetectable. Still, Olivia straightened her back. She wasn't used to men noticing her.

"Usually do your baking on Sunday mornings?" Zeke inquired.

It sounded like an innocent question, but she hadn't forgotten his invitation to attend church. "I don't have any set schedule. Just felt like a brownie day."

He held up what was left of the small brown square. "Works for me."

Olivia watched him as she sipped her coffee.

"Nice house," he commented.

She took in the living room as though seeing it through new eyes. Neat, tidy, not much more. She hadn't made any additional attempts at decorating after Ted was gone.

"You going to tell me why?" he continued.

Olivia swallowed. She knew he wasn't talking about the house. "I assume you mean my refusal to go to church?"

"Yes."

"It shouldn't be too difficult to figure out. This is a small town. I imagine you've heard what happened to my husband."

"We've got a grapevine for things that count, probably for some that don't. But no, all I know is that he passed on."

She laughed with a bitterness she hadn't been able to conquer. "*Passed on.* Sounds so gentle. Almost reasonable. Well, that wasn't the case. Ted was murdered. Does that shock you?"

"Of course it does. Never knew anyone who was murdered. What happened?"

Olivia repeated the details, regretting that she would never be able to stop telling the story. "So," she concluded, "the police told me Ted was in the wrong place at the wrong time."

"Small comfort."

Her laugh was still bitter. "Ted was the regular churchgoer. I grew up going to church sporadically. Mostly Sunday school or Vacation Bible School, but Ted was a believer. Made me one, too, for a time." Olivia met Zeke's steady gaze. "He lived what he believed and I saw how good that made our lives. Then for no reason…" Tears welled up in her eyes, but she refused to let them fall. "So you're wasting your breath trying to recruit me."

"Did I say I was recruiting you?"

"I won't go to church, Zeke. I appreciate your family's kindness today. But I'm not trading what I believe for Sunday lunches."

Zeke's eyebrows rose. "I don't recall anyone suggesting that."

Olivia gripped her mug tight. "But that's what you were getting around to. 'Come to church—see that there's a reason in everything the Lord does.' Well, there was no reason. Ted never harmed anyone. He was kind and good. And he died because God didn't watch over him. And there aren't enough Sunday lunches in the world to—"

Zeke took her arm so swiftly she stopped speaking.

"My mother meant what she said. We'd like you and Joey to spend Sunday afternoons with us. It's not a bargaining tool. That's not who we are. I asked you about church because I see something in you that I can tell hasn't healed." He paused. "Maybe it's from working with animals so long. I figured it had to do with the loss of your husband. I didn't know the awful way he died. Faith helps with that, but you have to be ready for it."

"Faith? So I can believe He'll watch over Joey like He did Ted?"

Zeke looked at her, his blue eyes so dark they were the color of the nighttime ocean. "It took me a long time to accept faith. That's how I know it works."

"So when I'm drowning, I don't try to help myself—I just assume the Lord will do it for me?"

"The heavier the burden, the more you need to relax, to float in those waters, knowing you aren't ever alone."

"I'm glad that works for you." Olivia inhaled, her breath almost painful. "But you haven't a clue. I'm not putting down the safe little town that Rosewood is, but you can't imagine how it is outside of here. How your world can suddenly turn black without even a moment's notice. And going to church isn't going to change that."

Zeke studied her face, his expression somber, searching. "You're that sure?"

She wasn't certain of anything anymore. Only that things would never be the same. "For me."

He lifted his hand, and two fingers traced the outline of her cheek.

Olivia felt a quivering that had nothing and everything to do with feelings.

Out of her depth, she felt those drowning waters.

And Zeke's fingers slipped beneath her chin, lifting it. "This conversation isn't over."

He rose and walked to the front door, then paused to stare into her eyes once more. Then he was gone.

But the touch of his hand on her cheek remained. As real as the feelings he'd stirred.

Chapter Nine

Nervous as a cat stranded in a tree, Olivia tried to get a grip on her anxiety as she drove to Zeke's. She'd rejected a hundred reasons why she couldn't go to the clinic, why she had to just drop off Joey and escape. Then she would remember her promise to Angie. And she couldn't get the image of Zeke's face from her mind. Or the impression of his hand cupping her face. Today school was out for teacher prep day, Joey wanted to go to the clinic and she couldn't think of a reason to refuse.

Olivia's cell phone rang suddenly, startling her.

Kate's cheery voice was miles away from her own mood. "Would today or tomorrow work for lunch? I know you'll have to see what's on the agenda when you get to Zeke's."

Olivia realized her thoughts were still jumbled and cleared her throat. "Sure. Today would be good, actually. What would you think about going to breakfast instead of lunch?"

"I'm adaptable. I've only had coffee this morning."

"I'll call you as soon as I check in with Angie, then," Olivia said, knowing she didn't want to face Zeke any sooner than she had to.

Luckily, Joey was wearing his earphones, listening to his music. She really didn't want to explain things. It was too much like running away.

The Tea Cart was even more charming than Kate had described. Maddie was warm and welcoming. The food looked tempting, but Olivia didn't have any appetite.

"Is everything okay?" Kate asked, laying her fork down.

"Why do you ask?"

"Unless you're churning butter, I think you've stirred that cream in your coffee enough."

Rattled, Olivia removed the spoon. "Just a lot on my mind, I guess."

"Feel like telling me?"

Olivia hesitated. Kate was a friend of Zeke's. It wouldn't be fair to talk with her about him. So she latched on to another topic. "It's Joey and my dad."

"I thought they got along well."

"They do," Olivia agreed. "But my father thinks Joey should go to military school."

Kate's eyebrows shot up. "Whoa."

"Exactly. Dad says that I don't discipline Joey enough, that he'll basically grow up to be a mess with only me for a parent."

"Ouch."

Olivia shrugged. "You've met him. The Colonel's direct."

"But military school?" Kate shook her head. "That's supposed to take the place of a father? Seems like it would make matters worse. Imagine how lonely Joey would feel."

"That's exactly what I think. He's down to one parent as it is. He's enjoying his community-service work. And I think he might apply himself more at school now."

Kate picked up her cup. "Have you considered the Community Church school? It's not lax, but it's a tight-knit group."

Olivia shook her head. "That's not an option."

Kate seemed puzzled for only a moment. "Ah."

"Yes, we don't go to church, either."

"Everyone's in a different place in their faith journey," Kate replied quietly. "I'm here if you ever need to talk about it."

"Seems like everyone is."

Again Kate's eyebrows rose. "Everyone?"

Flushing, Olivia wished she had an automatic lock that kept her thoughts from instantly converting into words. "That's an exaggeration."

"Hmm. Yesterday was Sunday. Church and the afternoon with the Harrisons. How many guesses do I get?"

Olivia felt sure Kate only needed one. "I think I might get a muffin after all."

"Sudden pang of hunger?"

"Kate, if something happened to Tucker, do you think you could ever be interested in someone else?"

The teasing disappeared from Kate's face. "I don't know. I wanted Tucker to be able to move on because I loved him, but…" She swallowed. "I've tried to put myself in his place a thousand times, and…I can't."

Olivia sighed. "Please don't say anything to anyone, especially Tucker."

"Done."

"I'm just confused, Kate. Ted was my whole world. How can I even think about replacing him?"

"You're not. No one will ever be Ted. Even though I haven't known you long, I sense you have a lot of love in you, enough for both Ted and someone else. Just because you're interested in a new man doesn't mean you stop loving Ted."

"I didn't say anything about love!" Horrified, Olivia covered her mouth. She was attracted to Zeke, but she wasn't in love. She couldn't be.

"No, but eventually, if you have feelings for someone, they may turn into love, and that's okay." Kate sighed. "Since I married a widower, it sounds like I have an agenda. But I didn't intend to fall for Tucker. The Lord brought us together."

Olivia pinched her lips into a line.

"I'm not trying to push my beliefs on you." Kate leaned forward. "Olivia, whatever it is that you're feeling, don't you imagine that Ted would approve? That he would want you to be happy?"

She'd never thought of it like that.

"Olivia, this isn't something you have to decide overnight. You have to get accustomed to the idea. To see if you can accept that your life isn't what it was when Ted was alive, that it couldn't remain exactly the same. We grow, we change. Even when we don't want to."

Was that even possible? Meeting Kate's sympathetic gaze, Olivia wondered.

"Dog run over on the highway," Angie told Zeke the moment he hit the office near lunchtime. "In surgery. I started an IV."

Zeke walked into the surgical area. A golden-retriever mix, the large dog was stretched out on the operating table, her breathing shallow. A cursory glance told him she had recently given birth. He didn't recognize the dog. Could be one of the unfortunates dumped in the country to "roam free." Most were hit by cars or slowly died of starvation. If she was a stray, she'd been abandoned too long.

"J. C. Mueller found her. He had rounds to make, so he couldn't stay. Said he'd pay for her care if she's a stray."

J.C. was the local neurosurgeon, an excellent doctor and an even better friend.

This animal couldn't be helped with a local and small incision. All indications pointed to internal bleeding. Which was fatal without surgery.

Angie finished x-raying the dog while Zeke scrubbed up. Speed was crucial. There wasn't time for any pre-op blood work. Angie administered the anesthesia while he shaved the dog's abdomen. A quick study of the X-ray confirmed his diagnosis.

Hearing quiet footsteps, he saw that Joey had come into the room.

He didn't have time for the boy. Without hesitation, Zeke picked up the sterile scalpel and made a clean incision. They could have used a third set of hands to suction the blood, but he and Angie had worked together long enough that they coordinated each motion. Hearing a gasp, he turned long enough to see Joey faint, fortunately landing on some cardboard boxes stacked by the wall. Seeing the internal organs of a dog splayed out on the table was a world away from seeing the small incision on the goat.

A few minutes later the outer door opened. Not long after, he heard Olivia calling all their names.

"Back here," he replied, his words muffled by the surgical mask.

Olivia stepped inside, surveying the room. Her gaze landed on Joey and she rushed toward him. Still unconscious, his face was slick with cold sweat.

One hand flew to her lips before she turned an accusing stare on Zeke. "He shouldn't have been in here."

"Helping out at a veterinary practice is more than petting kittens and playing with puppies," Zeke replied. "But to set the record straight, he came in here on his own."

She grabbed a towel, stuck it under the spigot and ran the cold water. Kneeling, she wiped Joey's face and neck. It didn't take him long to come around.

"Mom!" Mortified, Joey tried to sit up.

"You're the one who passed out," she reminded him quietly as she guided him back down.

"And we're still trying to save this dog," Zeke reminded her.

Olivia realized she hadn't properly assessed the situation or processed the implications. "Can I help?"

"Yes," Angie replied. "You can suction so I can assist Zeke."

Swallowing, Olivia nodded. "Joey, when you feel steady, can you watch the phones?"

"Yeah." Embarrassed, he didn't sound robust, but he was all right.

Olivia rushed to wash her hands and arms, then quickly pulled on a pair of gloves, a gown and a mask. Gingerly, she offered her hands and Angie guided them. Seeing what was needed, she closely followed Zeke's lead.

Her hand trembled, but she calmed herself, knowing the dog's life was at stake. Zeke was steady, unperturbed. She wondered how he was able to maintain his composure. Until now all she had seen of Zeke's expertise was on the surface as she helped out in the office. But now, with a life on the line, he reminded her of a soldier on a mission. Skilled, determined, unflappable…heroic.

Suppressing the rush of feelings, Olivia switched her focus to Angie, waiting for her to tell her when to suction.

Minutes passed like hours. Finally, Zeke wove in the last of the stitches.

"You can wash up now, Olivia," Zeke said, his attention still on his patient.

"Oh, right." Backing away, she pulled off the disposable

gloves and dropped them in a waste can. Remembering Joey in the other room, she slipped off the gown and mask.

Her son sat behind the desk, his expression anxious as she emerged. "Is the dog gonna be okay?"

"I don't know." Still mesmerized by the experience, she wondered that herself. "Zeke is…a really good doctor."

"Duh."

Reality returned with a thud. "I've never been in on an operation. Give me a break, okay?"

Joey cracked a smile.

And for a moment he was her Joey again. The carefree boy who had been filled with grins and laughter.

The phone rang. Joey looked at her in question. She nodded, giving him the go-ahead.

While he answered the phone and checked the appointment book, Olivia realized this was just another day for Zeke. No wonder he was so devoted to his practice.

Glimpsing the clock, she decided to make a fresh pot of coffee. Zeke would need it. And she needed to untangle her feelings.

It had been close, very close, but Zeke thought the dog might pull through. Sadly, her chances weren't good. Now, though, she needed more care and attention than his stretched staff could provide, but he would work something out. He pulled off his surgical cap and tossed it in the laundry, his mind now filling with thoughts of Olivia rather than of the injured dog.

The dog had been given everything Zeke could offer; not so much with Olivia. Amazed that she had stepped in, unflinching, to help, Zeke shook his head. He'd only expected her to retrieve supplies, pick up discarded dressing materials, but she'd plunged into the deep end. She had never come across as a delicate lily that would bend under pressure, but at the same time, he had been witness to a lot of vulnerability.

Not bothering to take off his scrubs, he strolled into the reception area. "Guess that blew a hole in today's schedule."

Angie shook her head. "Not as much as you'd think. We can reschedule a few appointments and not have patients here until midnight."

"And Angie needs to go home," Olivia pointed out, her eyes signaling to Zeke that he was about to get an argument.

"It's only a few extra hours—" Angie began.

"On your feet," Zeke replied, belatedly seeing that Angie looked pale, exhausted. "No arguments."

"But—"

"You're outnumbered," Olivia interjected, patting Angie's shoulder. "Even Wonder Woman got to disappear between capers."

Angie's grin betrayed her fatigue. "I feel like a total wimp."

Zeke shook his head. "You look like a glowing mother-to-be."

"Glowing?" Angie's eyes widened. "Not even if I was surrounded by fireflies, but thanks."

Chuckling, Zeke grasped the folder in Angie's hand. "Go."

"There's a lot of paperwork and if it's not done, the morning will be—"

"Go." Olivia chimed in with him. "I can finish up."

"You've got to make dinner for Joey and—" Angie protested.

"We can fix something to eat," Zeke told her. From the array of expressions, he'd surprised everyone in the room.

"Or get some takeout. I'll have to keep a close eye on our newest patient."

"I could grab some takeout from the BBQ Shack," Olivia offered.

"Who could say no to that?" Angie decided. "Will you get me one of their huge extra-sweet pickles and leave it in the fridge for me?"

"Extra sweet?"

"I know." Angie rolled her eyes. "I usually devour the sour ones, but now…" She patted the slight bulge of her tummy.

"With Joey, I wanted Mexican food for breakfast, lunch and dinner for nine months," Olivia confessed. "And anything with cherries—pie, strudel, turnovers. Quite a combination."

Laughing, Angie gathered up her purse. "I'm afraid I'm craving everything under the sun. By the time he or she is born, I'll barely be able to waddle."

Zeke suddenly thought about the newborn puppies from the stray. Were they lying somewhere in a field where their mother had been abandoned?

"Zeke?" Olivia prompted after Angie was gone.

"Just thinking. Joey, can you keep an eye on our newest patient while I pick up dinner?"

"But I was going to—" Olivia started.

"I have something to do while I'm out." He looked at Olivia. "Do you mind?"

"No, there's plenty to catch up on."

Zeke didn't want to mention the puppies in front of Joey. The mother had been in pretty bad shape before being hit. There was no telling what had happened to her litter.

Zeke counted off the mile markers until he found the one J.C. had noted.

Like most of the usually verdant fields, this one was dry,

withered by drought. Normally, patches of bluebonnets, Indian paintbrush and buttercups would be waving in the gentle breeze. But today those same soft breezes carried the charred scent of burned wood and wild grass. The fires were creeping closer every day. Austin was close to being ringed in by fire. He couldn't remember a time when the entire state seemed consumed by fire. From the Panhandle to Houston, drought had produced enough kindling to feed a thousand fires. And the number of fires, big and small, had exceeded that figure.

All sorts of wildlife had been driven from their habitats—those fortunate enough to escape the fires. But domestic stock was threatened, as well. The veterinary grapevine was filled with tales of overrun corrals and barns as wildfires swept through rural areas all over Texas.

The dry grass crunched beneath Zeke's feet as he scanned the field. Holding one hand over his eyes to shield them from the sun, he searched the ditch where J.C. said the mother dog had lain. Poor animal was probably trying to find food and water so she could provide for her pups.

In the midst of the brown field, something moved. Squinting, Zeke couldn't make out if it was a tumbleweed or perhaps a puppy. Wasting no time, he crossed the field. Zeke knelt down when he recognized the newborn pup, its eyes still closed. Carefully, he scooped up the tiny thing, already planning to wrap it in towels once he got back to the truck. "You have any brothers or sisters?"

The puppy mewed as Zeke continued looking. Finally he found the rest of the litter. It seemed the lone pup he held was the only one that had survived. Zeke nestled the little guy into the towels and made sure he was secure before he retrieved the others. He would bury them, but not out here where the coyotes would dig them up. Sadly, these weren't the first animals he'd had to bury on his small ranch.

Didn't take him long to make the trip back home. Certain that the rest of the litter was sufficiently covered so Joey couldn't see it, Zeke carefully carried the one puppy into the clinic.

Olivia's eyes widened when she saw what he held.

"Wow!" Joey exclaimed. "Did it just get born?"

"It's her pup," Zeke explained, gesturing toward the room where the mother had been moved. "I was lucky to find him."

"What do you need? For bedding?" Olivia asked, her eyes darkening in concern.

Obviously, she had guessed what had happened to the others but was wise enough not to voice it in front of Joey.

Zeke told her what supplies were needed. "This little guy will have to be hand-fed."

"Can I do that?" Joey asked eagerly.

Zeke looked at Olivia.

She wavered. "I suppose…."

Zeke knew he had to check on the mother dog. If there had been another option, he would have been steadily taking her vitals since the surgery had ended. "Then I'll hand him over now."

Joey's hands shook at first when he accepted the newborn. Olivia folded the soft towel so that it was doubled for extra warmth. For once her son didn't mind her help.

With the pup in safe hands, Zeke checked on the mother dog. Her vitals weren't good and she hadn't awoken from the anesthesia. If she awoke, the dog would have a long road to recovery.

"The BBQ Shack?" Olivia whispered, coming out of nowhere.

"Didn't know if any of the litter would survive. The mother's been neglected, probably dumped on the highway."

"So the rest...?"

He nodded. "I'll bury them later, after you and Joey are gone."

She shook her head. "Do you think we'd leave you with a critical patient *and* a newborn? We're made of sterner stuff than that."

"Olivia, this is what I do."

"I'm guessing Angie's usually around. And now that she isn't, you have to manage on your own. There's no need for that. After you get Joey settled feeding the puppy, I'll go pick us up some dinner. Looks like we've got quite a night ahead of us."

Chapter Ten

Olivia didn't exactly know why she had volunteered. It wasn't like her to be so impulsive. But behind Zeke's confident gaze, she could see that he had been affected by the plight of both the mother dog and her unfortunate litter.

It wasn't Olivia's responsibility to make him feel better. In fact, she was sure he had scores of friends who could help him, but in that moment, she'd felt needed.

The BBQ Shack loaded her up with brisket and side dishes. Another quick stop at the bakery and she tucked a pie, some cookies and some caramelized nuts beside the takeout. Luckily, there was plenty of coffee on hand at Zeke's. She was positive they would need it. Olivia frowned, thinking about Joey. Zeke would delay telling him about the sad fate of the litter, but at some point Joey would ask if there had been only the one puppy born.

In their house, anything connected with death had been deliberately avoided. She and Joey no longer watched mysteries on television or in the movies she rented. Not that she expected to keep him from encountering death forever, but these puppies... Well, this was very personal. Olivia checked the digital clock on the car dash. Fortunately, the usual lack of traffic allowed her to get to town and back quickly.

Entering the front door, she heard noise from Zeke's personal quarters. She sniffed, smelling a touch of hickory.

Olivia walked through the tall double doors to see a fire blazing in the large fireplace. Another glance and she saw Joey in one of the big chairs, the tiny newborn in his arms.

He looked up.

She kept her voice to a whisper. "How's he doing?"

"Okay, I think. Zeke let me give him his syringe of milk." Undisguised pride coupled with tenderness coated his words. He had always been a sensitive boy. It was only after Joey had lost his father that he had taken on his tough attitude.

"I thought you'd have to use a bottle."

"That comes later," Joey told her, using information he had no doubt just learned from Zeke.

She held up the bags of food, managing to raise her thumbs at the same time, signaling her approval. "I'll put this in the kitchen, get our dinner ready. Where's Zeke?"

Joey nodded his head in the direction of the clinic.

After taking time only to unload the food, Olivia walked through the back hall to Zeke's acute-care section.

He was checking the dog's heart rate. Hearing her, Zeke turned, his expression not giving away much. The fact that he had disguised his feelings told her the dog wasn't doing well.

"I wonder what her name is," Olivia said quietly. "She looks like a Carmie to me."

"Carmie?"

Olivia shot him a small smile. "It was one of the names I'd planned to give my puppy once I got one."

"Carmie it is."

"When will you know?" she asked, hating that she had to ask.

"Medicine isn't that exact. I'd say she was abandoned or lost at least a week before the car hit her."

Olivia flinched. "Poor thing. She was probably trying to find someplace safe to have her babies. Has Joey asked about the others?"

"I told him truthfully that I suspect some of them were stillborn. Without shelter or nutrition, they very well could have been. And with the temperatures we've had, she's so dehydrated it's amazing she didn't die giving birth."

"Can you guess her chances of making it?

"Maybe thirty percent." He paused, wiping his hands on a towel.

She flinched again. "That bad?"

"It's amazing she survived the surgery."

"What happens now?"

"We wait. Check on her, make sure she's stable and pray."

"Dinner's in the kitchen," Olivia said.

"And it's welcome. Didn't have time for lunch. Then with the surgery…"

Suddenly Olivia had a purpose, one to busy her hands instead of her thoughts. "I picked up brisket. I'm sure it won't be as good as your dad's, but I know it's a favorite. What about the puppy? Does he come back in here to the hospital part now that he's been fed?"

"Not yet. We need to keep hands on the little guy. Keep doing what his mother would have done. Then I'll put him in a heated incubator. But for now, the heating pad under the blanket's doing the job."

"I'm surprised the little thing's not shivering."

"Puppies don't develop a shivering reflex until they're two weeks old."

"Um…how about we make those plates and eat in front of the fire?"

"You and Joey don't have to stay. I told you—"

"And I heard you the first time." She shrugged, not wanting to admit how important it had become to her to stay and help him. "And you'll get the same answer. Do you like everything on your baked potatoes?"

He blinked.

"Because I got them with all the fixings. I hope Joey will eat one, but just in case I got potato salad and fries, too. And baked beans, of course. Plenty for all of us."

"You switch channels faster than a remote control," he remarked.

"Kind of thought I needed to," she replied. "Joey's putting his heart into this and I don't want to tread on it."

"That's what men's hearts are made for."

Shocked by his words, she stared at him.

He rubbed his brow, a weary gesture. "So we have brisket and baked potatoes?"

"Now who's the remote control?"

"Smells good," he said, ignoring her question. "And are those roasted nuts?" He reached toward the bag.

"Carameled," she answered automatically. "Roasted first, of course. Hey, why are we talking about food?"

He leaned close enough to whisper, "Because sound carries really well into the living room." His breath barely skimmed her ear, but she felt tremors from head to toe.

Forgetting about dinner, she trailed him as he took stock of the food she'd brought.

"I'll check on Joey," Zeke told her as he turned back toward her.

Olivia wasn't certain if she nodded, but she was positive she didn't speak. How could one tiny brush with him practically lift her off the ground?

The two voices blended from the other room. Zeke's deep and warm. Joey's tentative but growing stronger. Still mesmerized, she followed the sound.

"You don't need to whisper," Zeke explained to Joey. "He'll sleep through dynamite, especially right after feeding. Your mom brought dinner. Why don't you grab a plate while I hold him for a bit?"

"Can I wait to eat?" Joey asked, leaning forward earnestly. "I'm not hungry."

Zeke exhaled. "I'm not sure your mom would like that."

Coming back to earth, Olivia willed her voice to sound normal. "Just this once, I think it would be fine."

Zeke turned around, and when his eyes met hers, they filled with warmth, enough to scatter her wits again.

Heading back to the kitchen after him, she regained her presence of mind, then reached for plates. It didn't take long to fill them. Knowing her son enjoyed the caramelized nuts, she filled a small bowl with some, along with a few cookies.

"Dessert before the main course?" Zeke questioned.

"We don't often encounter newborn puppies," she explained. "It won't hurt him this once."

He smiled through his fatigue, a real smile. "I remember once when my mom let me eat a whole pie." His quiet chuckle raised the mood. "I'll never forget it. She makes those deep dark-chocolate pies—soft as silk and tastes amazing. Meringue's about three inches high. I was down in the dumps and she knew it, so she didn't stop me from polishing off the pie. Afterward I had the bellyache to prove it. But it was worth it."

She loved that his memories all seemed so kind and caring. "I really like your mom."

"And she likes you."

Olivia blushed, shaking her head.

"Don't be a stubborn wart, as she would say," he told her. "Mom doesn't invite just anybody to be a Sunday regular. Only special people."

"You're just saying that."

"Nope. As you saw, we have plenty of Harrisons to feed. Then there are old friends who are like family. But unless it's a party, Mom thinks that's enough. Without extra visitors, she has the time to visit with her grandchildren and friends."

Olivia cleared her throat. "It was very kind of her to include us. But we don't want to be a nuisance."

He chuckled again. "When you *really* get to know my mom, you'll realize she doesn't throw out Sunday-afternoon invitations that easily. I shouldn't tell you this, but Mom told me she sensed something special about you."

Olivia reached up to cover her blushing cheeks. "I've been told that before—" she paused "—that there's something different about me."

"There's certainly nothing ordinary about you," Zeke told her quietly.

Hesitating, she lifted her eyes, meeting the intensity in his, wondering. Olivia swallowed, her throat dry, her thoughts scrambled.

Zeke stood close, so close she could see the fine laugh lines around his eyes, the cleft in his chin, the tan on his skin that betrayed how often he was in the sun.

"Hey, Zeke!" Joey called out.

Olivia stepped back so fast she landed against the wall. "I'll grab our plates."

Zeke hesitated, reached out one hand, then let it drop. "Yep."

Olivia got hold of her senses, then put the finishing touches on their dinner plates.

* * *

"That's why we change the bedding often," Zeke explained as she walked into the living room. "And clean him up each time like his mother normally would."

"Is she going to be okay?"

Zeke exhaled. "Hard to tell, Joey. For now, though, the puppy's enough to concentrate on."

The fireplace, loaded with thick logs, put out considerable heat. Joey was situated in the chair closest to the blaze. "How do you know when it's too warm for the puppy?" she asked, putting her mug of coffee on the side table.

"He needs it to be ninety degrees," Zeke explained.

"Thus the incubator," she murmured.

"Might not think so, but he's lucky. Firstborn—the mother had enough energy to lick him thoroughly." He didn't add that not all of the others had been so fortunate. Not that he blamed the mother dog. Just the callous jerk who had dumped her. He was fairly certain that was the case because while the dog wore no collar, there was a crease in her ruff where one had been attached.

"Do you still put a clock in with a puppy to keep them company?" Olivia asked.

"There's no scientific proof it works."

Joey held up the hand with his digital watch. "He can use my watch."

Olivia and Zeke exchanged an amused glance.

"Don't think we'll need it," Zeke replied.

Olivia covered her grin and Zeke felt suddenly old. Joey was so young he didn't know anything about clocks that actually ticked.

Zeke sat back on the couch, stretching long legs into a comfortable position. He'd been on his feet for hours and was beginning to feel it. "If this gets out, I'll know who to come after, but I use a plush baby toy. One that mimics a heartbeat. Not all orphans take to it, but some have."

"Didn't know you were so well acquainted with baby toys," Olivia commented.

Realizing she was hiding a grin, he grinned himself. "I have a crop of nieces and nephews, remember? I know more about toys than any grown man should."

Her smile was soft. "Oh, I don't know. It's kind of nice. I bet you're their favorite uncle."

He shrugged. "Couldn't say. But it's a relief to hand them back to their parents some days."

Olivia stared down at her potato with unwarranted attention. "Ever think how it would be to have some you keep on a full-time basis?"

Only a million times.

The wood in the fireplace popped suddenly, more like an unexpected firework than a traditional crackle.

Seeing Joey's eyes dart to the tall, imposing mantel, Zeke explained, "That's the sound of the fire hitting sap in the logs. I don't mind the pops—sometimes they wake me up when I doze off in here." He shifted his gaze toward Olivia, imagining her tucked at his side.

"Zeke," Joey asked, "do you think we could put the incubator in here?"

Zeke scratched his head. "Hmm. We'll be using the smallest incubator. I suppose so. We've already given the little guy some oxygen but I want to keep the temperature and humidity consistent." A lot of newborn puppies didn't make it because it was simply impossible to provide the environment they needed. But Zeke had taken to using incubators for fragile puppies early on in his practice. He wanted each one of them to have the same chance of survival.

"Will his mother miss him?" Joey questioned anxiously.

"Not right now," Zeke replied quietly. "She's asleep." Unconscious, but Joey didn't need to know that.

"Does he miss her?"

Old hurts never completely disappeared. Although Zeke hadn't known his birth mother long, through every foster home, he had cried himself to sleep wishing she would return. "I think he's too young to miss more than feeling cuddled and secure. But we need to put him in the incubator pretty soon."

Joey held the puppy a fraction closer. "Oh."

Olivia watched her son, then turned to Zeke. He knew she was worried about her child, his obvious attachment to the fragile puppy. So far she hadn't even touched her dinner. Not that he'd made all that much headway into his. It was his job, a career he'd joyfully chosen. But he had never become calloused to the losses. Especially needless ones.

"We can put the incubator next to your chair," Zeke told him. "That way you can keep a close watch."

Olivia smiled at him, a smile that told of sweetness and maybe promise. And somewhere deep in his thoughts, he wondered what it would be like to have Olivia sharing his evenings, Joey in the picture, happier than he'd been since losing his father.

For all that Zeke distrusted his ability to judge women, he knew he wanted a relationship. Probably was the reason he'd gotten involved the last time, just as his dad had pointed out. He had been crazy about Penny's kids.

This was different. Joey was a great kid, but it was Olivia he was drawn to, Olivia who made him wonder if he could open his heart again.

Was it this crazy night, the emotion of everything they'd just gone through, the soft light from the fire that played over her face?

A loud pop zinged from the fire. But none of them stirred. And Zeke savored more than the moment—he savored the dream.

Chapter Eleven

Sunlight struggled through the dawn, slicing through the drapes, pushing back the layers of sleep. Indistinct sighs and the sound of stretching stirred the quiet air.

Joey flipped back the blanket Olivia had covered him with. Zeke lifted one booted foot and pushed aside the quilt that usually was folded in a leather trunk beside one bookcase.

Sensing the movements, Olivia opened her eyes. It had been a crazy night, between checking on the mother dog and feeding the puppy once Joey finally fell asleep. The little one had to be fed every four hours, tidied up, then placed in fresh bedding.

Joey came to life. "Is it time to feed him?"

Zeke glanced at his watch. "In about an hour."

"I'll make breakfast," Olivia said, stating rather than asking. Zeke literally had his hands full. Knowing they needed sustenance, she searched for and found the bacon and eggs and a large loaf of bread from the local bakery. Her own recipe for French toast wasn't as sweet as most and was very filling.

Soon the bacon sizzled on the stove and the coffee brewed, the delicious aromas wafting through the room.

"I don't know what you're cooking, but it sure smells good," Zeke commented, filling a mug with coffee.

She reached for the creamer, adding some to her mug. "I figured we all needed a hearty breakfast. Hope you like French toast."

"Even more than buckwheat pancakes," he replied with a smile.

Warming inside, she returned his smile. When had she last reached out to help someone? Giving instead of worrying only about her tiny family? "Um…I'm cooking bacon, too. Think that'll be enough?"

His eyes darkened into a deep ocean-blue.

Was there something more to his expression? Or was that wishing thinking? Aware of her son close by in the next room, she busied her hands with the egg mixture. But she couldn't resist peeking to see what Zeke was doing. When she did, she was startled to meet his gaze.

Zeke inclined his head toward the hospital. "I'd better check on our patient."

Olivia's stomach did a two-step as she watched until he was out of sight.

"Mom?"

Nearly jumping out of her shoes, she turned. "Morning, sweetie. What is it?"

Puzzled, he stared at her. "Huh?"

"I mean what do you think of French toast this morning?"

He lifted one shoulder in a partial shrug. "S'okay. The puppy's still sleeping."

"I think they do that most of the time when they're first born. I never had a puppy, but babies sleep a lot."

"I wonder when he'll open his eyes."

"I think that we could use a book on dogs."

"Zeke'll know," Joey replied assuredly.

Touched by the confidence Zeke evoked in her son, Olivia swallowed the worry crowding into her thoughts. Were she and Joey becoming too involved in his life?

Just then Zeke returned. "Joey, how about checking on the puppy?"

"Sure."

Sobered, Olivia stared at Zeke. "How's the…?"

"It won't be long. I've got pain meds in her drip, but she's unconscious."

Olivia looked toward the living room.

"I can tell him," Zeke offered.

She hesitated. "I don't want to burden you with this."

"It's never easy, but I've had to deliver this kind of news more times than I want to count. Usually, it's older pets. There's no good way to tell people their animal is gone, but I can assure Joey she's not in pain."

Olivia's lips trembled. "Death's still hard for me to deal with."

His eyes filled with understanding. Then he turned toward the living room.

She felt like the worst coward. But she couldn't drag herself into the other room. Telling Joey about his dad had been as bad as the loss itself. Hurting him again… She just couldn't.

Zeke assessed the situation in one glance. Joey sat on the floor, his gaze glued to the incubator where the puppy slept.

"Few puppies get this kind of round-the-clock care," Zeke began, lowering himself into the closest chair.

"Is he supposed to sleep this much?" Joey questioned anxiously.

"Yes. Until he's a little older, all he'll do is eat, poop

and sleep." Zeke smiled gently. "That's enough to wear him out."

"He sure is a swell puppy," Joey said with longing.

Zeke wondered if Olivia would allow the boy to keep the little guy. "He's in good shape, too."

Joey stared up at him. Trepidation filled his young face. "What about his mom?"

"She's not doing as well." Zeke thought of the unfortunate dog. "Her injuries were massive, Joey. I think she's stayed alive long enough to make sure her pup was okay."

Joey stared at him, his eyebrows furrowed together. "Then…she'll be okay?"

"I'm afraid not. She was in bad shape when we got her."

Joey's face fell. "But you're a vet. You could fix her."

Zeke lifted his hands, turning them palm-side up. "I did everything I could. I promise you that."

"It's not fair!" Joey all but shouted. A single tear escaped and he wiped it away in shame.

"Joey, never be embarrassed about caring for animals. If her owner had cared about her, she would never have been hit by a car, because she wouldn't have been on a highway fending for herself."

"God's mean," Joey declared in a less defiant but still assertive voice.

"God doesn't want His creatures hurt. He cares for the smallest sparrow. But people have free will, and when we make bad choices, like her owner did, bad things happen."

"My dad never did *anything* bad!"

"Of course he didn't. I don't claim to understand why things happen the way they do, but I know the Lord was watching over this little puppy. He shouldn't have survived, but look at him, sleeping, knowing nothing yet but sweetness."

"But he won't have a mom."

"He has us."

Joey's shoulders slumped, along with the rest of his body. "I never get to have real pets."

Zeke didn't want to make any promises he couldn't fulfill and couldn't guess whether Olivia would let him keep the puppy. "For now, let's just be glad he's safe, warm and being fed."

Olivia lurked at the doorway, having overheard most of the conversation. Imagine, a man so attuned he could speak of sweetness and sound masculine at the same time.

"Breakfast is ready," she announced, making extra noise as she walked through the arched doorway. "Will the puppy be okay alone while we eat?"

Joey looked suddenly panicked.

Olivia didn't give Zeke a chance to answer. "Zeke, do you suppose Joey could have a plate in here so he can keep an eye on the puppy?"

"Sure."

Not wanting to see either of their expressions, Olivia fled back to the kitchen. She filled a plate for Joey, adding the extra syrup he always wanted.

"I'll grab a glass of milk for him," Zeke said quietly from behind her.

"You got in here fast," she muttered.

"Not as fast as you," he retorted mildly. "It's a puppy, not a baby lion."

"Oh, Zeke, what if something happens and that puppy doesn't make it? Joey will be devastated."

"First, I think the puppy will make it with the right care. But more important, you need to realize you can't keep Joey from every ugliness in the world. Of course you want to protect him. I didn't want to have to tell him about the mother dog. I wish I could have pulled off an impossible feat. But that's not always reality."

"So the Lord wasn't watching over the dog?"

"Have you always lived in a black-and-white world?"

Olivia blinked.

"Because I haven't." Zeke paused. "I'll take Joey his milk and then I'd better check on the mother again. I don't want her to be alone when... I don't want her to be alone."

"Is she in any pain?" Olivia practically whispered.

"No. She'll go in her sleep."

"Zeke, how do you do this time after time? Doesn't it break your heart?"

"It's the ones I can save that make it worth this."

Olivia carried Joey's breakfast into the living room, pausing to study him. He was already in love with the tiny puppy. It was written in every posture, every movement. What should she do? Should she let him risk being hurt? Or had the bubble she'd tried to create around him already cracked?

Sensing her presence, Joey turned to look at her.

Smiling softly, she knelt on the floor beside him. "I can help watch him while you eat."

"I'm not very hungry."

Risking rebuff, she gave him a small hug. For the first time in nearly a year, he didn't pull away after mere seconds. She swallowed. Hard. "I put extra syrup on your French toast."

He accepted the plate. "It'll be time to feed him pretty soon."

"Then it's a good thing you're so handy with the syringe."

"You're not going to make me go home to sleep?"

"Would you sleep at home?"

"Nah. But—"

She shrugged. "So no point trying. Besides, he might miss you." In that moment, Olivia knew she had to let him keep the dog. The two belonged together.

"Thanks, Mom."

She squeezed his arm again. No longer feeling like flotsam swept along a rushing river, Olivia knew they were taking a risk. But it was time to take control, to let Joey be a boy again, to not fear each step he took, every action, every breath.

Forgetting about her own breakfast waiting in the kitchen, she watched the tiny puppy along with Joey. In a way, it reminded her of when Joey was a baby, so small and helpless, a bundle of pure joy.

Zeke unhooked the final intravenous connection. The dog, as he had predicted, never awoke. It was some comfort to know she hadn't been in any pain.

Sighing, he peeled off his gloves and tossed them in the trash. He hated to face Joey, knowing how disappointed he would be. It had become personal, he realized. Any boy would be upset to learn the dog hadn't made it. But Joey wasn't just any boy. Not now. It wasn't just his change from being sullen. Zeke had gotten to know him, seeing his grin when he accomplished something, noticing how he genuinely cared about the animals. And knowing he was Olivia's.

Closing his eyes for a moment, he envisioned the ray of sunshine she had been at the last Sunday-afternoon gathering.

With that picture weaving through his thoughts, he left the house, picked up a spade and started digging the grave. It wouldn't take long. With each spade full of dirt, Zeke wondered if Olivia would let Joey have the puppy. And how was he going to get her out of his thoughts?

If only she had a shred of faith left. He'd known people who had been raised without faith, others who had lost theirs because of some trauma, often a loss. But not anyone with both. He could offer his support, but she would have to reach for her faith, to believe, to let the Lord into her life.

By the time he finished digging the grave, he'd worked up a sweat. Wiping his forehead with the back of his hand, he stared out over his land. No matter what he told his dad, his life would never be complete without a woman he loved at his side. He wanted a wife, children. Someone to share the joys, the sorrows, the triumphs.

Zeke retrieved the mother dog and the pups that hadn't survived and placed them together.

"Goodbye…" What had Olivia called her? "Carmie. You didn't deserve this fate, but on the other side, you and your pups are running in the sweet wild grass."

He filled in the dirt and tamped it down, then covered the space in rocks, a final layer of protection. He didn't mark the grave. He didn't need to. He remembered each animal buried in the plot.

Back at the house, he entered through the kitchen door. Two full plates remained on the counter. Funny that Olivia hadn't eaten. After washing up, he walked quietly into the living room. Olivia was stretched out on the rug beside Joey.

The boy looked up, then placed a finger against his lips, warning Zeke to be quiet.

When he was close enough to hear Joey's whisper, he pointed to Olivia.

"She was pretty tired. Wanted me to stretch out. Then she did and…" Joey raised his shoulders in a small shrug.

"We better let her sleep. On one condition. Eat your breakfast."

"But—"

"You want me to wake her up?"

Grudgingly, Joey reached for his plate.

"Go stick it in the microwave," Zeke instructed. "I can watch the puppy."

Joey studied him for a moment, then apparently decided Zeke was qualified. "Okay."

Instead of watching the dog, Zeke studied Olivia. Asleep, the tiny furrow of worry between her eyebrows disappeared. Her mouth curved in a natural smile, as though she had reason to laugh. He couldn't see her eyes, but he knew they were violet, like gems plucked from a treasure chest.

Honey-blond hair fell slightly over one cheek. Giving in to the impulse, he gently brushed it back.

Olivia stirred slightly, then settled.

Good thing. How would he explain that gesture?

The squeak of Joey's shoes alerted him to his return.

"You didn't eat, either," Joey said as he sat down.

"So I didn't. Better heat mine up, too." It was with great reluctance that he stood and moved away from Olivia. *Sleeping Beauty* was supposed to be a fairy tale. Perhaps he was beginning to believe in magical fables, as well.

Chapter Twelve

The school term sped to an anticlimactic end. Joey was so invested in the puppy and its welfare he didn't even acknowledge that his community service was officially over.

June had blown in hot and dry when it normally would be a gentle beginning to summer. The usual wildflowers that populated the hills and meadows were meager, ravaged by the bone-dry conditions that hadn't let up in the Hill Country.

Drought consumed the entire state from the Panhandle to the Gulf Coast. Fires had begun popping up everywhere. So far they remained primarily contained, but Zeke worried that it might not last.

Standing in his parents' backyard staring at the cloudless sky, he worried about the consequences of a lasting drought.

"Penny for your thoughts," Olivia said quietly.

He turned, surprised. "I thought you were in the kitchen."

"Your head's in the clouds," she teased gently. "I could have ridden out here on horseback and you wouldn't have noticed." She studied his face. "Something wrong?"

"No. Just thinking about the weather."

"It's hot, that's for sure," she replied, lifting her hair from her neck.

He was tempted to capture that wave of hair, to kiss her ivory skin. Instead he agreed, "We're in for a scorcher of a summer."

Olivia glanced over at the kids kicking the soccer ball around at the end of the yard. "Doesn't seem to bother them."

"They're young."

"Said Methuselah," Olivia teased.

He felt old. It was finally time for a decision about the puppy. Even now, Joey wasn't playing soccer with the other kids. Instead he sat beneath the wide, spreading magnolia tree, the puppy in the portable incubator beside him. Zeke had warned him that he had to keep the little guy clear of the younger children, who might play too roughly.

"It's time, Olivia."

Her expression dimmed. "What do you mean?"

"Are you going to let Joey keep the puppy?"

Her mouth opened, but no words emerged.

"Joey's falling more in love with the pup every minute he spends with him."

"But the puppy's still so fragile."

"Life is fragile," he reminded her quietly.

"You think I don't know that?"

"I think you know that far better than most people. You tell me. Would you rather not have had the time you did with your husband? Would you have changed things, never married him if you'd known he would die young?"

"That's not fair!" The pink of her cheeks rose from anger rather than the heat of the day.

"Life isn't always fair. You and Joey know that much, much better than most people," he replied.

"So because Joey's already suffered, it's all right to

hurt him again?" Anguish filled her words, etched itself in every line of her body.

Zeke longed to take her hands, to pull her close, to tell her he would never let anyone hurt either of them again. "Olivia, do you really believe I want Joey to get hurt?"

She shook her head.

"Then can't you try to trust that it will turn out okay?"

"I knew the very first day that they belonged together," she confessed. "But the puppy is so fragile," she whispered.

Like her heart. He knew it as well as he knew the color of her eyes, the smell of her golden hair, the breath she was holding.

"What if something happens to him?" she pleaded.

Something already had—to his heart. "Can't you trust me?"

Violet eyes deepened to the darkest purple. "You're so sure?"

"I'm sure Joey needs to do this, to make this puppy his own."

Olivia gazed across the yard, her face filled with love and concern. Hesitantly, she took a step forward.

Zeke followed as Olivia approached her son. Joey barely looked up, his gaze fastened on the puppy.

Olivia tucked her skirt over her calves as she sat down on the grass next to Joey. "So how's he doing?"

Joey's defensiveness was all but gone. "Sleeping."

"He does a lot of that, huh?" She ruffled Joey's hair. "I remember when you were that young you slept a lot, too."

"Mom!" Joey glanced up at Zeke, mortified.

"She's just stating the facts," Zeke told him, leaning against the tree. "We all start out as infants."

"One thing was different, though," Olivia remarked casually to Joey. "You had a name on day one. He's almost four weeks old and we're still calling him 'the puppy.'"

Joey looked down. "I wasn't sure I should give him a name."

"Why not?"

Joey lifted one shoulder, then let it drop. "'Cause it oughta be the owner who gets to name him."

Olivia slipped an arm around his shoulders. "Then you'd better start thinking of a name."

Joey's expression turned incredulous. "You mean I...?"

Olivia smiled. "You two belong together, don't you think?"

Forgetting he was nearly a teenager, Joey launched himself into her arms, hugging her tightly. "Mom!"

She hugged him back, relishing this rare gift.

"I'll do all the work, taking care of him, I mean. I'll feed him and walk him and clean up after him." Joey rattled off a string of related chores.

Olivia realized he would promise the moon if it meant keeping the dog. Funny how such a small stranger could capture so much of one's heart. Maybe Joey felt a bit as she had when he was born. One minute a baby was mostly just a concept; the next it was the most important thing in a person's life.

"Did you get anything to eat?" Olivia questioned.

"I had some chips."

"Your puppy won't mind if you eat some lunch. Zeke and I can watch him while you fill a plate. And before you ask, yes, you can bring it back here to eat."

Joey ran to the long, wide tables.

"Keep this up and you'll be mother of the year," Zeke teased. "You won't regret it, you know."

"I'll remind you of that next Mother's Day."

He'd like to think she would still be part of his life when

that holiday rolled around. But for now, he had today. And he didn't intend to waste it.

Joey returned with a plate and a can of orange soda. He scarfed down the food as though he hadn't eaten in weeks, so Olivia laid a hand on his arm. "Slow down."

"But it's almost time to feed him," Joey explained.

Zeke checked his watch. "Not for half an hour. Listen to your mom. Food digests better when chewed."

Joey rolled his eyes but slowed down somewhat. "He gets really hungry. You can tell."

The puppy made tiny mewling noises . Zeke chuckled. "Joey's spending so much time with him, he can tell just when the pup starts getting hungry." He extended a hand to hers. "Ready to get something to eat?"

"Sure." Automatically she accepted his hand, feeling that special twinge that happened only with his touch.

Nancy Harrison hadn't needed to pressure her into coming to the lunch—because Zeke had arrived at her house after church to drive her to his parents' home. And the lure of being able to bring the puppy along in the portable incubator was something Olivia couldn't fight. Not when she saw the longing on her son's face. A quick trip to Zeke's clinic to retrieve the puppy, the incubator and an extra-long extension cord, and here she was.

The Harrisons had greeted her casually, as though she'd attended these events for years. It was still new, the feeling of being so accepted. Because she'd spent her life wishing she could belong, it wasn't something she could casually accept.

"Aren't you hungry?" Zeke asked.

She looked at her empty plate. "Um, just waiting to see everything."

He pointed at the end of the last table, where they stood. "You know of some hidden grub?"

"Guess my mind was somewhere else."

"On a little boy and an even smaller puppy?"

Grasping her plate, Olivia sighed. "Busted."

"Joey senses how tense you are, and it makes him fearful. Haven't you guessed that's why he's so full of bravado?"

Had she pushed her child into an untenable situation?

"Come on. Let's put some food on that plate." He steered her toward a plate of honey-glazed chicken wings, baked beans and salad, then held her elbow as they found a spot at one of the many tables scattered around the yard.

It was only after she sat down that Olivia realized they hadn't returned to Joey's side. She craned her neck to see him.

"He'll be fine," Zeke reassured her. "And it'll give him a chance to show off his dog to the other kids."

"I suppose so." She laughed, a soft sound as her lips curved upward. "I wonder what Joey will name him."

"Oliver?"

She stared at him. "Oliver?"

"The feminine of Olivia." Only the twitch of his lips gave away his amusement.

She pretended to consider the name. "Well, I am the one who's allowing him to keep the puppy…." Unable to hold it in, she started laughing. "Oliver? You're as bad as Joey."

"At what?"

"Teasing." As she said it, Olivia realized that Joey had begun teasing her again, a sign of normality. "Wow."

He held up one hand in protest. "I never claimed to be a comedian."

"I don't know. You have your moments. Actually, I was realizing that Joey's started teasing again, acting—" she shrugged slightly "—well, normal."

"People assume that younger people bounce back from a

trauma sooner. And I suppose that might be true for some kids. But I know it's not always that way. What happens when we're young can leave an awfully deep imprint."

"That's encouraging," Olivia replied in a downhearted voice as she put down her fork.

He leaned forward. "I'm saying that while everyone reacts differently, it's important they get a chance to move on, to deal with what happened. And that's not possible in a bubble. Joey may compare the puppy's fragile state to how strong his dad was, wondering how if one didn't make it, the other can. On the other hand, he may concentrate only on the puppy, and when he's strong again, he could reflect on how life is unpredictable."

"I'm not sure how I feel about that."

"For me, it's knowing I have faith to lean on that gets me through," he replied quietly. "I know that's not what you want to hear, but not everyone can get through a day without it."

"That's pretty much what Kate said," Olivia admitted. "Especially since her husband was a widower."

"Tucker's genuine, one hundred percent. Ask Kate about his faith. It might help."

"I don't know how. There are a lot of the faithful here in Rosewood and—"

"Just ask," Zeke persisted.

She looked toward Joey. "It occurs to me that you've talked me into more things than anyone in...well...anyone."

He smiled that grin of his that made her melt. "Really?"

At that moment she suspected he could talk her into almost anything. How strange. The only other time she'd felt that way was with Ted.

"Mom!"

Startled, she dropped her fork. Zeke was already on his feet.

He tapped her shoulder. "It's okay. Joey is smiling."

Her heart rate was still galloping as she rose and crossed the yard.

"Look, Mom, Zeke! His eyes are open!" Most puppies' eyes opened after two weeks, but the fragile newborn hadn't opened his eyes until the fourth week.

Olivia crouched down beside him. "Are his eyes really blue?"

"Cool, huh? He'll be like one of those Arctic dogs."

Zeke chuckled. "They're born with blue eyes, but they eventually turn brown."

Joey scrunched his eyebrows together. "Are you sure?"

"Yeah. I'm sure."

"Then I want to call him Brownie," Joey decided on the spot. The puppy fastened his gaze on Joey. If love was visible, it poured from the dog to her son. They had bonded the first moment Joey had held him. Now his adoration made it crystal clear. Olivia wanted so much to make sure that the puppy would be okay and that her son wouldn't have his heart broken.

"You wanna hold him?" Joey asked.

Very carefully, Olivia accepted the fragile bundle. The sweet puppy smell reached her nostrils just as Brownie licked her hand. Utter sweetness. They should have let Joey have a pet sooner, she thought. There had always been excuses, but at the moment she couldn't think of anything more important than this connection.

"Isn't he great, Mom?"

Olivia smiled. "The best."

"In a week or so he'll probably be out of that incubator," Zeke said.

Bubbles could only last so long, Olivia realized. And when the cracks began, there was no telling what would come next.

Chapter Thirteen

A week passed and Joey was more in love with Brownie than ever. The dog seemed to be either all wiggles or sleeping so intensely nothing woke him.

Olivia checked through the day's appointment schedule. Angie was experiencing a serious bout of morning sickness, so Olivia had volunteered to handle the office for a few days. Not a trained tech, Olivia had to send the blood samples to a vet in Fredericksburg, but that was a small inconvenience.

The door opened and Olivia smiled when she saw that it was Kate. "Hi!"

"Hope I'm not interrupting."

"Interrupt away. I'm up to my elbows in accounts. Do you have time for coffee?"

"Absolutely. I thought I could smell it brewing."

Olivia headed toward the kitchen. "Coffee should be just about done. I was driving by the bakery and smelled their doughnuts, so we have something to munch on. What brings you out this way?"

"You mean since I don't have a pet with me?"

Olivia laughed as she took down two mugs. "I didn't mean to sound that way."

"I hoped to catch you before you got too busy."

"Something up?"

Kate held out her mug. "Well, I don't know." Then she looked at the doughnuts and frowned.

Olivia filled the mug with the fresh brew. "Is anything wrong?"

"Not exactly."

Olivia smiled. "They're the zero-calorie doughnuts, provided we don't confess that we ate them."

But Kate didn't share her smile. "I'm already feeling guilty. I'm not sure I ought to add calorie guilt." She tapped the side of her mug, then met Olivia's eyes. "I feel like I'm being a tattletale or a gossip, and I've never been fond of either."

Puzzled, Olivia drew her eyebrows together. "I don't know many people well enough to gossip about them."

"You know this one."

"My father?"

"I'm afraid so."

"You might as well tell me, because chances are he'll get around to saying something anyway. I'd rather be prepared."

"I did a few sketches of him the last time we talked. I felt I hadn't really gotten the essence of him." Kate hesitated. "Like he was all locked up."

Olivia sighed. "He always has been."

"I thought maybe if we talked about Joey, he would loosen up—you know, brag like grandparents do—and I'd see another side of him."

Olivia's stomach suddenly knotted. "What did he say?"

Kate glanced down, then gripped the handle of her mug. "He's trying to arrange a scholarship to a military school for Joey. He thinks no one would turn down an opportunity like that...not even..."

"Me," Olivia finished for her.

Looking miserable, Kate nodded. "I don't know if he'll even be able to get something like that done. But I know how you feel about Joey staying with you. And look how he's flourishing here at the vet clinic. I've never seen such a turnaround in a kid. It's like he's another person."

"You really see the difference?"

"You don't?"

Olivia and Kate stared at each other for a moment.

"You're around him every day, so it's probably hard for you to see it," Kate continued. "He's been changing this whole time. Believe me, he's not the same kid he was when I first met him."

Olivia didn't know what left her more befuddled. She had never believed her father could change and he hadn't. But she realized she hadn't given Joey enough credit for the change he had accomplished. "I'm amazed. Not by my father. If it were legal, he'd already have Joey in military school. But Joey… To me he's always been a wonderful kid. I knew when he was acting up it was because he was hurting. I just didn't realize he had come so far, enough for you to notice."

"You're a great mom," Kate reminded her.

"I can't take all the credit. Joey acts differently around Zeke. He respects him."

Kate smiled. "Zeke's a good guy. Most people think he'd make a great dad."

Embarrassed, Olivia stirred her coffee, fumbling with the spoon.

"You need to keep those eyes open," Kate replied. "Listen, I still feel weird about telling you what your father said, but…"

"I've lived with his attitude my whole life, Kate. It hurts but I suppose I'm not really surprised."

Kate snagged her arm. "Olivia, I know how you feel about your relationship with the Lord—"

"Relationship? There isn't one."

"However you want to phrase it. Olivia, I'm praying for you. For you and Joey. I know what your father said must hurt. And…" Kate gazed down for a moment. "We don't understand why everything happens. But without faith, it's so much harder to cope."

Olivia knew Kate was talking about her wish for a baby that hadn't materialized. "I'm glad you have your faith to lean on, but I'm not going to change."

Kate sighed.

Immediately, Olivia felt small for not accepting what Kate offered. "But I suppose prayers can't hurt."

Kate's eyes began to water.

Olivia realized Kate was fighting back tears. She had shut God out of her life like closing an ill-fitting door. But she could see how much Kate's faith meant to her, that it really did sustain her.

"Kate, I don't have what you, Zeke and so many other people seem to take for granted. But I'm deeply touched that you want to help me with your prayers."

Kate impulsively hugged her. "This will sound nervy, but I sense a seed of belief in you. And I sure understand why you'd be angry because of Ted's murder. I'll be the first one to admit I don't understand His plan all the time." Unconsciously she glanced at her flat abdomen.

"Yet you still believe?" Olivia asked, wondering how Kate achieved such peace.

Kate met her gaze. "Someone once told me that our relationship with the Lord can mimic one with a person we love. We might get awfully upset with them, even think we hate them when things go wrong, but in the end that love doesn't falter." She lifted one shoulder in a partial shrug.

"I might want to kill Tuck in the morning for something he's done, but nothing is as good as seeing his face when he comes home for the day."

"But if something happened to him?" Olivia had to ask.

"I'd be heartbroken. But I'd try to remember how broken he was when I met him, how much love he still had to give."

Olivia grasped Kate's hand. "I hope your prayers all work out."

Kate's expression spelled out her understanding. "I just have to be patient. And if a baby isn't in the plan, I have my beautiful daughter."

Olivia squeezed her hand. "I don't know why, but I have a feeling *your* prayers are going to be answered."

Kate smiled gently. "Then we'll both be happy."

"I've lived all over the world and I've never made a friend so quickly. Thank you." Olivia stumbled over the last two words.

"You'll have to move away to get rid of me," Kate responded, sounding more like her usual self. "Now, we've probably let our coffee get cold."

"Not to mention ignoring the calorie-free doughnuts," Olivia replied. Picking up their mugs, she stuck them in the microwave. As they rotated, her own thoughts circled. Kate had given her a lot to chew on. More than a whole plate of doughnuts would cover.

Zeke knew his land the way parents knew their children. The fields that tucked in his outbuildings, the slope of the hill that curved on the western boundary line. Normally, the wild grasses would be thigh high; bluebonnets and Indian paintbrush would dot the fallow land. But the rains hadn't come.

And the wildfires were increasing. Every day brought

reports of new outbreaks. The brush was dry, the sky cloudless. The only storms were dry ones that brought lightning to torch the land but not enough moisture to be called even a drizzle.

The animal-rescue-sanctuary grapevine was buzzing. Zeke knew the growing number of displaced animals was staggering.

"Whatcha doing?" Joey asked, his arms full of now-twelve-week-old puppy.

Zeke turned around, then hid a chuckle. "If you don't ever let his feet touch the ground, Brownie's going to get paunchy."

Joey frowned. "Are you serious?"

"He needs exercise," Zeke replied kindly. "Use the smallest leash and he can walk with you out here."

"I thought all the stickers might hurt his paws."

"It's rougher than normal, but his pads will adjust. Walk him mostly on the dirt trails for now. He needs to toughen the pads, and walking keeps his nails from getting too long."

"You cut some dogs' nails," Joey observèd.

"Mostly older dogs or those who don't get enough out-door exercise." Zeke's soft spot for the boy was deepening. When they had first met, Joey had been all anger, pain and disappointment. Again, so much like himself at that age. But the layers were stripping away.

The boy had a natural touch with animals and Brownie had only strengthened that. But he was also sensitive, a good thing in Zeke's estimation. Too many preteens and teens thought being macho was important. Remembering his own tough attitude as a teen, Zeke could only shake his head.

"What?" Joey questioned, seeing the movement.

"Just thinking," Zeke replied. "That's why I like the

quiet. Most people can't understand. They're so busy chasing excitement and fun they can't feel the happiness you can only sense from inside."

Joey stroked Brownie's ears. "I feel happy when I'm around Brownie."

"That's natural. We always feel better when we're near the ones we love, people or puppies. And when you have one special love, like Brownie, it's better than extra cherries on a banana split."

"Do you have someone special like that?" Joey asked innocently.

"Oh, I have a mess of family," Zeke said, trying to shift the direction Joey was taking. "They give me more love than I need."

"Hmm." Joey pulled his eyebrows together, thinking. "But not *one* special person?"

"Not exactly."

"Don't you want to?"

Zeke decided Joey was entirely too insightful for a twelve-year-old. "Maybe. Sometime."

"My mom used to have my dad," Joey said in contemplation. "Do you think she needs someone?"

Zeke wished he could back the conversation up to before he'd gotten Joey on this track of thought.

"Maybe another puppy?" Joey continued. "He could be friends with Brownie and me but be Mom's special dog."

Zeke chuckled. "I think one puppy at a time is just fine." So Joey wasn't ready for his mother to join the dating game. Zeke couldn't help wondering how the boy would react if a man *did* enter Olivia's life. Would he resent anyone who threatened to take his dad's place?

"You never said. Whatcha doing out here?"

Zeke tipped his face up toward the sky. "Smelling the air."

"'Cause of the fires?"

Zeke frowned. "What do you know about the fires?"

"Everybody's talking about 'em. One of the guys said Rosewood's going to burn down."

Beneath the casual words, Zeke sensed fear. "I won't tell you the fires *can't* reach us, but it's unlikely they'll push into the town. The brushwood's been cleared. The wind carries smoke and ash a long way. The closest fire is about sixty miles away and they're getting it under control."

"What about the animals that live out here and in the woods?"

"The wild animals try to outrun the fires and a lot of them make it. But the horses, donkeys, cattle and sheep that are fenced into corrals don't have that option."

"What happens to them?" a worried Joey asked.

"I belong to horse, donkey and mule recovery groups. We offer land and corrals for people to bring their animals to. I'd take in cattle, sheep and goats, as well."

"Do they all escape?"

Zeke wished they could. Desperate owners, unable to transport their animals, had opened corrals and stables so the animals could make a run for it. Unfortunately, fires were blazing in every direction. But Joey didn't need to be burdened with the knowledge. "Owners do their very best. Sometimes neighbors move as many as they can, sort of like carpooling. And there are sanctuary groups like the ones I belong to. I've offered all the corral space I have to animals that need to be relocated."

"What would happen if the fire *does* come here?"

"I don't worry about things that I don't expect to happen. I'd rather help the people and animals who *are* having trouble."

"Zeke?"

"What is it?"

"How did the sky smell?"

As though the fires were marching closer. "About the same as yesterday. Now, you've got a puppy to walk, and I need to check out today's appointments."

Olivia sat at the reception desk, her face grim as she listened to someone on the phone. She waved Joey toward the back and Zeke knew whatever it was, it was serious. She hung up not long after Joey was out of sight.

"Well, tell me," Zeke said.

"Austin's fires are worse. Same thing in Bandera. They don't only need corral and barn space. They need volunteers to help handle all the stock that has to be moved." Olivia raised her amazing eyes, now filled with concern. "You didn't tell me that you belong to *all* these groups."

"It never came up before," Zeke responded truthfully. And it wasn't as though Olivia were his girlfriend or fiancée, someone he would automatically confide in. But the look on her face...

"But what if you have to go help?"

"It's not *if*—it's *when*."

Shock seized her expression. "Zeke!"

"They need every hand they can get," he explained and told her about the veterinary network.

"But won't they need you more as a doctor?" she all but pleaded.

"There are injuries in the field. They're desperate for vets."

"But what about all your patients here?" Olivia demanded.

"I've spoken to a few of the vets in Fredericksburg. They'll take my patients until I get back."

"But... "

"What, Olivia?"

"Why *you?*" The last word was barely a whisper.

"Why not me?" he replied gently. "If not me, who?" He clasped her arms. "Olivia, I know the Lord will keep me safe."

"It doesn't work that way!" she blurted out, a tear sliding from one eye.

Immediately, he leaned closer, using his thumb to wipe away the tear.

"You big, stupid, hardheaded *man!*" She choked out the words with no anger or defiance. Her hiccuping sigh was peppered with tears yet to fall.

"Why are you getting so upset?" he questioned, wondering if he dared think it was more than friendly concern.

"I don't want you to get hurt…or worse."

"Why?"

Olivia's eyes were a deep violet and her lips trembled. "I…I just don't, that's why."

Zeke took her hand. "Is that the only reason?"

"Do you have to go right now?" she asked, swallowing. "I mean, can't you help but not be one of the first ones?"

"I'd hardly be one of the first to volunteer," he said. "Volunteers have been helping since the first fires started. But now it's in our neck of the woods."

"Why aren't the vets in Fredericksburg and the other little towns volunteering?"

"A few have, but that doesn't affect my decision. I'm going to do the right thing, regardless of what others choose."

Olivia stared at him. "What if it's more important for you to stay here? To take in refugee animals?"

He had battled with that decision. "The first group should arrive tomorrow. And I'll stay here long enough to settle them in. But I intend to help on the front lines, as well."

"And if the front lines come to Rosewood?" she asked fearfully.

"Then I'll be here."

"Do you promise?" Olivia asked, killing him with her jewel-like eyes.

Reluctantly, he nodded. An hour earlier he was convinced he was going to the front lines right away and nothing would stop him. But he hadn't counted on Olivia's reaction. Or the look in her eyes.

Chapter Fourteen

Olivia clenched the pen in her hand so tightly it left an impression in her palm. What was wrong with men? Willing to walk right into danger without a second thought. In a way, Ted had done the same thing. She hadn't wanted to leave Austin. And if they hadn't, he would never have been on that street in Atlanta. But he'd thought he was invincible. And now Zeke was literally volunteering to walk into the fire zones.

Unlike the Colonel, Zeke hadn't thoroughly dismissed her concerns. Still, she felt as though she were back in her army-brat days, worrying that everything familiar would be ripped from her.

Staring into space, she bit her lip, determined not to cry. Instead she squeezed the pen tighter.

The door opened and for the briefest moment, Olivia dropped her head. She didn't feel up to speaking to or dealing with anyone.

"Olivia?" Kate questioned, obviously concerned. "Is something wrong?"

"Oh!" She exhaled. "Thank goodness it's you."

"Why? Who were you expecting?"

"No one. Anyone." Olivia rubbed her brow. "Sorry I'm not making sense."

"That's okay. I don't make a habit of being sensible myself. But you're so pale. Can I get you some coffee? Or juice?"

"I'm not sick, Kate."

"Oh, then what's wrong?"

Olivia glanced toward Zeke's office.

Kate caught on fast. "Actually, I think fresh air might do the trick. Come walk with me for a few minutes."

Olivia looked again in the direction of Zeke's office. "I suppose he can answer his own phones for a few minutes." She pushed the rarely used intercom button and told Zeke she was stepping outside.

She and Kate left the office and wandered toward the barn.

"I'm not sure why, but I've always been drawn to barns," Kate said. "I've drawn sketches and sketches of them but I've never gotten around to painting one. Zeke keeps his up so well it doesn't have that worn look that some take on."

Olivia's breathing eased. "Thanks. Guess I really did need some fresh air."

"Without ears to pick up every word. So what's going on?"

Olivia recapped the situation. "And he said it's not *if*— it's *when*."

"Olivia, that doesn't mean he's going to dash out in the next ten minutes. I've known Zeke a long time. He's not going to abandon his own animals and critical patients."

"But he says he's already volunteered."

"Would he be Zeke if he didn't?" Kate said.

Olivia searched the near-cloudless sky. "He's going to be just as needed for the wounded animals."

"He's a pretty intelligent fellow. I'm guessing he factored that in. Olivia, just because Ted found himself in a terrible place doesn't mean Zeke will. He believes the Lord will take care of him. I do, too. Amazing the difference that makes."

"Are you saying that Ted didn't believe enough?" Olivia asked defensively.

"Of course not! I'm saying they are two different situations. I won't pretend to know why some things happen, but I do know that you don't need any more loss. And I don't think you'll have more. Zeke's not ready to literally throw himself into the fire. And, practically speaking, the firemen won't let him. But I can see how a veterinarian would be essential to the survival of a lot of trapped animals."

Olivia swallowed, and when she spoke, her voice was low. "I didn't think the fires could ever reach Rosewood."

"And we don't know that they will. Everyone's working hard to keep that from happening."

Sighing, Olivia reached for the top rail of the corral. "Tomorrow we'll get our first refugees. I imagine they'll be frightened."

"I think we're all going to be frightened until this fire season ends," Kate mused.

"All?"

"Remember, Tuck's the sheriff. That always puts him on the front line."

"You have a backbone of steel, Kate."

"Infused with Jell-O," Kate confessed. "I just have to trust he'll be all right."

Trust? Faith? It all seemed wrapped in an emotional equation. And Olivia had never been very good in that department.

But for the moment, just one moment, she wanted to believe.

* * *

Pickup trucks hauling horse and cattle trailers began arriving in the early-dawn hours. Zeke expected as many as his fenced acreage could accommodate, but the long line of trucks was still disconcerting. Some of the animals had been relocated several times. One group originated in the Panhandle, far north and west at the top of the state. Railed flatbeds held sheep and goats.

And for each vehicle, there was a heart-wrenching tale of what they'd been forced to leave behind—some had seen their homes destroyed as they fled. Plenty of Rosewood's families had offered refuge for the owners. The small bed-and-breakfast was doing its best to squeeze more people into the available space. Its parlor was now filled with cots. As were the church hall and the school cafeteria and gymnasium.

Zeke offered his living- and dining-room quarters, and a grateful family was near tears as they accepted.

Olivia arrived just after dawn. The day before, she and Zeke had gone over a system to keep animals and their owners connected. Immediately, she launched into cataloging animals and their corresponding owners. Touched by the tragedy that hit so close to home, she seemed to understand why Zeke had volunteered. Not that she had come to terms with it, just that she could see why he felt so compelled.

Horses, mules, donkeys, sheep and now goats. A mother and her five-year-old daughter, Tina, looked bereft as they unloaded a trailer filled with miniature donkeys.

"Will Pansy be okay?" the little girl asked anxiously.

The mother stroked the child's hair, clearly trying to hide her own fear and misgivings. "I'm sure she will. These nice people are good to all animals."

"But Pansy's special," Tina replied, close to tears.

"She's helped raise Pansy since she was born. Now Pansy's mostly a pet. But hotels don't think so." The woman sighed. "I don't suppose there's a hotel in Rosewood that's not full?"

"No hotels in Rosewood," Olivia replied. "One bed-and-breakfast and it's full, but there are still some spaces available at the school and church. Also, some homes." Early that day, Olivia had enlisted Kate's help to prepare a list. She had copies that she'd been handing out to those who asked. "Will your husband be joining you?"

"No, it's just Tina and me. Her father passed away before she really got to know him."

And before Olivia could restrain the impulse, she said, "I have a small house, but I do have an extra bedroom. It's not fixed up, but we have sleeping bags. You and Tina are welcome to stay until we know what's going to happen with the fire."

"But you don't even know us," the woman protested, a spark of hope in her eyes.

"I know you need a place to stay. You look exhausted. For now, why don't you and Tina go into the clinic? If you're hungry, feel free to raid the fridge."

"That's awfully generous of you."

"Well, generous of Dr. Harrison." Olivia made a mental note to stock up on Zeke's groceries, since she was giving them away.

The woman grasped her daughter's hand. "Thank you. I've been driving for days now, and I was afraid to find out what was going to be at the end. I'm sure glad it's you."

Touched, Olivia watched her for a few moments, then turned her attention to the next horse trailer.

The day sped by quickly until finally the fenced fields, barn and stables were stuffed full. A long line of trucks were still waiting in hopes of finding refuge. Zeke had to redirect them to Fredericksburg.

As the vehicles left, Zeke stood in his driveway watching.

And Olivia watched him. She knew him well enough to know that he wished he could take everyone in, that he had space for them all.

Zeke turned just then. And as sure as she was standing there, Olivia could read the intentions in his face. He was leaving. Soon. And there wasn't a single thing she could do.

Zeke checked over all the animals they had accepted. Olivia carried a clipboard, making notes while Joey watched intently, listening to Zeke's instructions. Luckily, they all seemed in good health. A few had signs of early-stage dehydration that could be taken care of easily.

Olivia felt terrible wishing one of them needed Zeke's attention. But she knew that wouldn't stop him. He would turn an injured or sick animal over to another vet.

Unable to sleep the night before, all Olivia could imagine were towering oak and pine trees ablaze falling on Zeke.

Her eyes felt as if they were filled with sand. She rubbed at them again.

"All the animal dander getting to you?" Zeke asked.

Olivia shook her head, not wanting to admit the truth to Zeke or to upset Joey. "I think it's just something in the air."

No sooner than the words were out, Olivia jerked her gaze to meet Zeke's. The air was filled with remnants of smoke the wind had carried their way.

"What if I run into any trouble?" Olivia asked, desperate to keep him from leaving.

"I've given you all the phone numbers to contact the area's vets. I'll carry my cell phone but I don't expect it to be reliable. The towers are overloaded with people trying to find their families and friends. The radio-transmission contact is going to be the most reliable. Joey, could you grab some more tags?" As Joey ran off, Zeke clasped Olivia's arms. "I'm counting on you to be the strong one here. Angie can't. I have volunteers lined up to feed and water all our refugees. You'll be fine."

"I still don't understand why *you* have to go," she pleaded.

He searched her eyes and Olivia saw the concern... and what looked like more. "I'll come back in one piece."

"You don't know that!"

"But I do. I have faith."

Olivia's chin dropped to her chest.

Gently, he lifted her chin so he could meet her eyes again. "The Lord will keep me safe."

"This is like all my childhood moves rolled into one day," she confessed. "Just as I almost thought I could fit in, we'd move away. Now you're going away, taking all that with you."

"You belong here, in Rosewood," he chided mildly.

"I've never belonged anywhere," she said without self-pity. "I've made a few friends, but if I disappeared tomorrow, no one would even miss me."

"Oh, trust me, Olivia, you would most definitely be missed."

Her heart skipped a beat.

"I wish you could see what I do," he continued. "Determination, kindness." Zeke paused. "So much more than I can say."

Olivia wanted to press him for the words, but she could hear her son running toward them.

Out of breath, he stuck the tags out to Zeke. "There aren't many more left."

"That's okay. We don't have a lot left to tag."

A wealth of words left unspoken whispered in the rising breeze.

Looking down, Olivia wondered at what Zeke had said. And what he hadn't. She wanted to ask. Instead she followed Zeke into the barn. Joey kept up a lively chatter, so she didn't have to make casual conversation. Grateful, Olivia knew it would have been beyond her.

It wasn't fair, having this happen twice in a lifetime. And how was she going to say goodbye?

Chapter Fifteen

"Moping won't help," Kate said before popping a freshly baked kolache in her mouth. "Raspberry, my favorite." She had brought the pastries to the clinic, since Olivia couldn't leave now that she was handling the place by herself. Angie was still under orders for full-time bed rest. And Zeke... Zeke had left.

Olivia hadn't touched her plate, though she had drained her coffee cup. "I didn't know it showed."

"Um, yes. You look like you lost your best friend."

"Actually, you're the best friend I have," Olivia admitted. "I suppose that seems kind of pathetic, since I've only known you a matter of months."

"Friendship isn't based on time but on a connection. I felt it the first time I talked to you about the portrait. And I'm honored to be your best friend. But I'm also worried about my best friend. Zeke isn't reckless. He's not going to go charging into the flames. He knows people here count on him, too. His family would be devastated. Especially because he's unique in their family dynamic. You know, because he was adopted."

"Adopted?" Olivia croaked.

Kate frowned. "You didn't know?"

Olivia shook her head.

"He was about twelve, I think. A total mess of a kid. Angry, rebellious, headed for serious trouble. Of course, that was because he was bounced from foster home to foster home, more than a dozen since he was five."

Swallowing, Olivia tried to take in what Kate was telling her.

"I didn't live in Rosewood then, so I only know what Tuck has told me. But he's not prone to exaggeration. Zeke's mother abandoned him when he was barely five.

"He didn't act up at first when he went into foster care, thinking she would come back for him. Unfortunately, the first foster parents couldn't keep him for more than a few months. And the second home was a terrible environment. You know, the kind of people who foster kids only for the money and take out their frustrations on the kids."

Olivia gasped.

"A social worker saw the bruises," Kate continued, "and he was removed, but the damage was already done. From then on, he was determined to rebel before new foster parents could hurt him. And that led to disruption after disruption. The foster families felt he couldn't fit in and kept giving him back. By the time he got to Rosewood, he was considered beyond redemption."

"That's horrible," Olivia murmured, shocked.

"But the Harrisons were as unique as Zeke, in a good way. He got in trouble repeatedly, but they just loved him more. When he finally realized that they were going to keep him no matter what he did, he started changing.

"Didn't hurt that he had older brothers to keep him in line. Not to mention Erica." Kate laughed. "She made Zeke her duty. She came on like one of the Furies if anyone tried to hurt him." Kate paused. "Zeke never told you *any* of this?"

Olivia's thoughts were swirling with all this information. "I wonder why he didn't. I was pretty callous when I told him about my moving around in the army, told him it was something he could never understand." She winced.

"How could you have known? To see him with the Harrisons now, you'd never guess how it was."

"They all seem so close," Olivia muttered. "I envied what he has." Struck by that truth, her fingers flew up to cover her mouth.

"Perfectly normal that you should have taken things as they appeared. I had a hard time believing it, as well. He's not biologically a Harrison, but he is in every other possible way."

Olivia then blurted out the first thing that came to mind. "Do you think his past is why he's never married?"

"No. Just a bad history with women." Kate hesitated. "Are you sure you want to hear this? I don't want to color your feelings about Zeke."

"How can the truth change that?"

"Zeke's not the kind of guy who would want you to feel sorry for him."

Olivia's eyebrows rose. "What do you mean?"

Kate sighed. "The first girl thought it was *cool* to date a bad boy, strung him along all through college, then dumped him."

"That's rough, but was it enough to make him give up on women forever?"

"He dated, just not seriously. Then he dated a divorcée with kids. Ultimately, she decided to give her marriage a second chance. Tuck said that Zeke was bitter about the first relationship, but that the second soured him on ever getting involved with anyone again."

Olivia couldn't hide the consternation she felt.

Kate took her hands. "That doesn't mean he still feels

that way. Men are funny creatures. So in charge and force-ful until it comes to their hearts. Then it gets pretty dicey. Zeke's seen his parents and siblings enjoy happy mar-riages, but he probably still remembers the mother who never returned."

"That's so…" *Reprehensible, unforgivable, unimaginable.* And Zeke had lived through it all. "But he seems to truly belong here in Rosewood."

Kate agreed. "It took a long time, I hear, but yes, he be-longs. Unlocking his heart is a little trickier. Would it upset you if I told you he watches you constantly when you're at the Sunday meals? When you smile, his eyes light up."

Olivia blushed but brushed it off. "I think you're let-ting your imagination run away with itself. I don't get it, Kate. Zeke talks about how strong and deep his faith is. How can that be after all he's been through?"

"How could he not? The Harrisons live their faith and that's what got through to Zeke, let him have the peace he needed so badly."

Olivia rubbed her forehead, trying to understand ev-erything Kate had told her. And to reconcile it with the man she knew only as generous and kind. Zeke a bad boy?

The phone rang. Olivia gave the caller information on the vet to contact while Zeke was gone.

"Kate, if Zeke hadn't left, I wouldn't be here alone." Olivia stared at the plate of Czech pastries. "I wonder if Zeke would have ever confided in me."

"When the time was right," Kate ventured. "Or if he was sure of your feelings."

"*My* feelings?" Olivia croaked.

Kate sighed profoundly. "I may have to take on the job of being a translator for you two."

The phone rang again and Olivia had to consult her

list. Some of the vets were so full from carrying Zeke's load that they were asking her to stop referring patients.

"You seem to be handling things here pretty well," Kate commented.

"I'm really just handling the phones. Volunteers are caring for the animals. Joey's helping, too. I think his puppy's going to wind up as a herding dog. He tries to herd every animal out there. We don't have any animals in the kennels—they were all outsourced to different vets. So no one needs to be in the clinic at night. Zeke's brothers and sisters and some friends are on a rotation for the nights in case anything goes wrong with the refugee animals. There are a few long-term patients in the barn, but their owners keep checking in on them. The word's getting around about Zeke being gone. The Rosewood grapevine?"

"Probably." Kate hesitated. "A lot of people are worried that the fire will reach us."

Shocked, Olivia stared at her friend. "Do you think it will?"

"I don't know. It would be wise to make an evacuation plan for your house, though. I'm guessing Zeke made one for the clinic and your guests."

"Yes. I have copies tacked up in the stables and barn and every room in here. I haven't thought about my house. I suppose I'd take family photos, a few sentimental things."

"It would be a good idea to get them packed in your car now."

Olivia's mouth opened. Trying to gather her composure, she picked up a pen. "I suppose I should make a list."

"I'm not saying I think the fire will reach us. But living with Tuck, I've learned not to take anything for granted. It's just best to be prepared, then feel relieved when you wind up not needing to leave."

Olivia briefly wondered if her brain could implode from

information overload. "I feel like an ostrich with my head hidden in the sand."

Kate smiled sympathetically. "You mean because I spilled Zeke's entire history in one coffee break?"

"I needed to know," Olivia admitted, although she still felt mean-spirited to have played "poor me" about all her moves now knowing what Zeke had endured. While Olivia tried to make a list, she couldn't help but ask Kate, "Why do you suppose Zeke never told me about his past?"

"He knows you're vulnerable about your past, too. He can understand better than anyone else. I can't imagine him wanting to hurt you more by telling you his story."

"That makes sense," Olivia conceded. But Kate's words rang in her mind. *When the time was right.* Would that really ever come to pass?

The knot of emotions in Olivia's stomach was roiling. She had just gotten off the phone with her mother, warning her to prepare in case of evacuation. As it always had been, her mother said she would discuss it with the Colonel. Which meant he would have the final say whether they would prepare to leave or not.

Worried he might get stubborn, Olivia wondered if she should try to talk to him. But history had taught her that might be just the wrong thing to do. He could dig in his heels just for spite, to show who was in charge.

Her mother had urged Olivia and Joey to come stay with them. Olivia had refused. She was afraid if something did happen, she'd be at the clinic and that would delay evacuating.

Zeke's mother had insisted that Olivia and Joey attend the Sunday-afternoon lunch and had threatened to come pick them both up if they weren't in attendance. After learning so much about their family history, Olivia felt as awkward as she had the times she'd walked into a new classroom. She shared a look with Joey and reached for the latch.

But the gate swung open and Zeke's mother, Nancy, pulled them inside. "There you are! I was about to come get you. How about some fruit punch? Erica won't tell us her secret ingredient, but it's very tasty."

The Harrisons smiled, nodded or waved as they walked toward the table filled with punch, soda and coffee. The smell of brisket permeated the yard. Zeke's father's specialty. Olivia wondered if he had chosen to distract himself with the barbecue. He had to be worried about Zeke, too.

As she glanced around the yard, it hit her. They must all be worried about Zeke. Still, they were carrying on the tradition of Sunday lunch. Was that what faith was about? Holding on tight to what you knew and even tighter to what you hoped?

Erica approached and Olivia instantly thought of what Kate had told her. Zeke's defender. She would never have guessed.

"Dad's cooking brisket," Erica said in greeting. "And the boys are already rounding up a soccer game."

Joey didn't need any more encouragement, leaving to join the game.

"Olivia, I want to thank you for being such a star while Zeke's gone."

"All I'm doing is answering phones, directing traffic. No heroics."

"Or worry?" Erica asked, her eyes knowing.

"I'm worried," Olivia admitted, not able to tell how much Zeke's siblings were worried.

"Zeke will get through this," Erica assured her.

"That's what everyone keeps saying."

Erica's eyebrows lifted. "Everyone?"

Olivia blushed, realizing her gaffe.

"The town grapevine," Erica continued, saving Olivia from having to explain. "We have prayer call chains, so half the town's on the phone with each other almost every day. Doesn't take long for news to get around. And Zeke affects a lot of people, with his practice, I mean."

"You think he's really safe?" Olivia ventured.

"Yes. I'm saying extra prayers for him," Erica said, "but I know the Lord will keep him safe."

"How can you *know?*" Desperation, frustration and hope battled in her heart.

"Because I have faith." Erica clasped her hands together. "It's not a panacea—it's belief, certainty in that belief."

"I wish I could be so certain," Olivia confessed, envying the faith that buoyed Erica and all of the Harrisons.

"It requires giving up some of the control you're accustomed to."

"My life has been all about control." Olivia thought of all the rules the Colonel had imposed on her life. "I'm programmed that way."

Erica smiled. "The Lord gives us free will. And I'm certain He expects us to be in control of our daily actions. Can you imagine the highway if we weren't the ones in control of our cars? Silly comparison, I know. But I'm better at having faith than explaining it."

"Actually, it's the best explanation I've heard." Olivia hoped that Erica's faith was well placed, that Zeke was under the Lord's protection. She glanced upward toward the heavens. Was God truly watching over them? And would He watch over Zeke?

Chapter Sixteen

Zeke stepped out of his truck, stretching to ease his muscles. He was one large ache. The long hours had been tiring, but treating fearful large animals took its toll even more. He'd been through a physical and emotional battering.

Man, but the ranch looked good. Despite the crowded corral and grazing acres and the strange animals filling them. There might be a faint tinge of smoke in the air, but it still felt fresh compared to the stench that had remained in his nostrils all the while he was near the fires these past three weeks.

And his house. Never had he appreciated the sight more. Awaiting him was a shower and soft bed. Sheer luxury.

The door opened as though he had willed it.

"Zeke!" Olivia shouted, rushing down the stairs, then running toward him.

His weariness and aches fell away. Squinting his eyes to make certain he wasn't dreaming, he took a step forward, then another. "Olivia?"

Midway between the house and the truck, they came face-to-face.

"You're all right!" Olivia exclaimed in a wondering

voice. To prove it she clasped his arms as though making certain he was real.

"Said I would be," he replied gruffly, undone by her caring.

"I know, but…you're really, really okay." Her eyes were blinking back tears.

His heart opened. "Couldn't disappoint you, could I?" He wanted to tell her that he had carried her face in his thoughts each waking hour that he had been gone. But he wasn't sure she was ready to hear those words.

She smiled with relief, but her lips still trembled. "I was so scared that… It *is* dangerous in the fire zones."

So much so, he couldn't tell her the extent of the damage, the constant press of heat that felt as if it were scorching his skin even though he was taking care of animals, not fighting the blaze. "So I hear," he said instead.

"Here I am babbling on, and you must be exhausted." She released his arms and he immediately felt the loss of their connection. "What do you want first? Something to eat? A hot shower?" She cast her eyes down, her face flushing. "Um, I mean, I'm guessing you're exhausted," she repeated. "And we have everything taken care of here. Our animal refugees are all fine. Dr. Wardle came by and checked on them early this week."

Before he could stop himself, Zeke reached out to cup one side of her face. He lifted his hand to touch her hair, then trace the curve of her cheek. She looked so good, so right, so beautiful with her exotic violet eyes and honey-colored hair. "Zeke?" she whispered.

Leaning in, he let his lips graze her temple. Vanilla and cherries, he thought, smelling her hair.

With deep regret, he pulled back, needing to see what was in her eyes.

Now the deepest amethyst, they called to him. He read

her vulnerability, a host of questions, but nothing concealed. Nothing that promised one set of feelings while hiding another.

Touching the back of her neck, he pulled her close again, inhaling her sweet scent. Ever so gently, he touched his lips to hers.

She paused only a moment before returning the kiss. Her lips were as soft as he'd imagined and filled with the promise he was seeking.

She kissed him as though she wanted the contact as much as he did.

Reluctantly, so very reluctantly, he eventually pulled back, then rested his forehead against hers.

They hadn't needed words. Not that he didn't want them. Words that would connect them in a permanent way. Words that would somehow let her know how he felt.

"Olivia," he finally breathed.

Her arms were still wrapped around him. "I've been so terrified."

He could feel her rapid breathing.

"I was so afraid something would happen to you. You're big and strong and capable, but—"

He placed two fingers against her lips. "It's okay to worry. I worry every time you and Joey leave the clinic to go home."

"You do?" she asked.

"Every single time." He picked up a lock of her hair and caressed it between his thumb and fingers. "So soft."

"I'm not helpless," she protested quietly.

"You're the most capable woman I've ever met. You're a survivor." He looked away for a moment, reflecting on his disastrous relationship record. "I am, too. I'll tell you about that sometime. I know how hard it is to survive. And you've done it in a strange town while raising Joey. Don't you know how amazing you are?"

Olivia glanced down, overcome with his compliments. "I don't feel amazing."

"Amazing people rarely do." He smiled gently.

Feeling as though she were in a dream, Olivia carefully touched the growth of hair on his chin, then inched up to feel the laugh lines by his eyes. Knowing what he had been through in his life, she was struck by how much laughter he'd been able to give. Always giving, this man. Always caring. "And you're the *ordinary* type?" she finally responded, halting the rush of words collecting inside her.

He grinned, that winsome smile she had liked from the first day they met. Then he took her hand.

They had shared a kiss. But his hand holding hers made her blood heat and she was certain her face was a rosy shade of pink.

"You're like a flower," he remarked. "Budding, then blooming."

Her first response was to wave the words away. She let herself enjoy them instead. "What kind of flower?"

"A rose. Definitely. And it's not clichéd—it's classic. An American Beauty."

Olivia felt as though she were in a dream. "You're going to make my ego swell until I'm impossible," she warned.

Zeke shook his head. "Nope."

"Oh, Zeke, you must truly be tired. We should get you inside and—"

"It's all good." Placing an arm over her shoulders, Zeke led them both to the house. "Joey here?"

Shocked that she had completely forgotten about her son, Olivia stumbled over the words. "He's in the barn, cleaning stalls."

"You two been okay here these long days?"

"Joey doesn't want to leave when it's time to go home. And I kept thinking that one day, you'd pull into the driveway and everything would get back to normal."

Zeke suddenly hesitated.

"What? What is it?" Olivia asked.

"Didn't even make it into the house," he muttered.

"Zeke?"

"The fire's moving closer," he admitted.

"Closer? To Rosewood?" Olivia blinked rapidly, thinking of all the implications. "Just by the highway?"

"Fires have sprouted up all over the Hill Country," Zeke explained. "They're wide and long, pushing through the fields and woods."

"You mean straight at Rosewood?" Horrified, Olivia felt immediately protective of her adopted town. "There must be something they can do."

"Firefighters and local governments are doing everything possible. But no one can control Mother Nature. Dry lightning sparks fires faster than they can mix the slurry to dump on them. Every hand will be needed to dig a firebreak along the borders of town."

Olivia swallowed a dry knot of dread. Then it hit her. "That's why you came back."

Zeke took her hand. "I told you if I thought you were in danger, I'd be back in time to help."

"So…" she began uncertainly.

"But that's not why I kissed you," he asserted. "That was about you and me. Not the fires."

"You're sure?"

"Positive. I thought so before I left. While I was gone, well…I realized what an idiot I'd be not to make certain that you're part of my life."

Overwhelmed, Olivia couldn't believe everything was happening at once.

"What's wrong, Olivia?"

She swallowed again. "Just taking it all in."

Zeke frowned. "From the look on your face, you don't like what you're thinking."

She managed a smile. "Actually, I—"

"Zeke!" Joey skidded to a stop, just short of a body slam. "You're back!"

Brownie barked and ran around both of them, circling happily.

"Mom! Cool, huh? We can get patients back and everything'll be like it was before."

Zeke met her eyes over Joey's head. No. Nothing was going to be exactly as it had been before.

The Harrison house had always been the best place to retreat. Especially on the porch swing out back. After a busy afternoon, Olivia and Joey had gone home. Not too much later, Zeke had headed here.

He knew what he had seen on Olivia's face. The same look he had seen twice before in his life. The look that said a permanent relationship wasn't in the cards.

His gut ached. He could still smell the sweet scent of her hair, feel the softness of her skin.

How had things gone so wrong so fast?

The screen door to the house creaked open. Erica stepped outside. "Hey, little brother."

He rubbed the painful indentation between his eyebrows. Great, his mother must have called out the troops.

"Glad you're back," Erica continued as she sat down beside him on the swing, "in one piece."

"I'm not a smoke jumper." Men and women who parachuted into fires that the rest of the people were fleeing. Rough, dangerous job. "Or a firefighter."

"No, but from what I've been following on Facebook and Twitter about the Texas fires, that put you in danger all the same. The horses and donkeys you treated weren't burned by candles."

"I'm okay, Erica."

"You seem awfully down. Coming back to the ranch usually makes you happy."

"Did Mom call you?"

"She called all of us. She was worried sick the whole time you were gone. Why? Did you want some private time?"

He laughed humorlessly. "As though that exists in this family."

"Aren't you precious?" Erica responded with her normal bite. "When did you get too good to have your sister welcome you home?"

"Mom really didn't send for you?"

"No." She looked puzzled for a moment. Then her big-sister protectiveness kicked in. "Why? What's happened, Zeke?"

"Nothing happened. That's the problem."

It took her only moments. "Olivia," she stated.

"Guess I'm more predictable than I realized."

"Spill," Erica demanded."

Zeke exhaled. "What if I don't want to spill?"

"You want me to sic Mom on you?" Erica threatened.

"Go right for the throat, why don't you?" He thumped his forehead. "You'd think by now I could recognize the women who aren't for me."

Looking puzzled, Erica tilted her head. "You mean Olivia?"

"Any other women in my life?" he countered.

"She's perfect for you," Erica responded. "I wish you could see what a perfect pair you two make."

"Funny—guess nobody told her that."

"You've got to give me more, little brother."

Zeke's thumb and forefinger gripped his jaw. Then he sighed. And told her about the events of the afternoon. When he finished, he expected sympathy. Instead Erica said, "You idiot."

"Well, thank you."

"You're single. Olivia is a widow and a single mother. Don't you imagine when her toes touched the ground after your kiss, she realized she had to think about her son? About her family? That doesn't mean her feelings for you changed. It means she has a lot to be concerned about. What if Dad died? Would you be ready for Mom to re-marry in a year or two?"

"They've been married forever. Not the same at all."

Erica rolled her eyes. "A year, fifty years. When one parent dies and the other remarries, it's hard for the children. Especially when they like the new spouse, because that makes them feel guilty. After all, this parent is taking the place of their deceased one. Is any of this getting through that thick noggin of yours?"

"You didn't see her eyes," Zeke replied quietly.

"I'm guessing there was some fear, trepidation, uncertainty. All normal."

Zeke shook his head. "Remember, I've tried this twice before."

Erica swatted his hand. "Not the same thing at all. You can't compare your past relationships with this one. How about thinking like Olivia? Try to picture how you'd handle telling Joey about the two of you."

He hated to admit it, but Erica could be right. Still, how

did he broach that with Olivia? And what if his sister was wrong? He already had two strikes against him. One more and he was out. For good.

Chapter Seventeen

Clearing the brush and digging trenches was hard, exhausting work. Yet nearly the entire population of Rosewood turned out. Men, women, teens, some children—all were battling to save what was theirs.

Early on, the closest brush had been cleared away. But the size and intensity of the nearby fires had proven too large for that to now be effective.

Now the volunteer fire department was talking about a controlled backfire on the other side of the trenches to remove all the dead brush that would fuel a major fire.

The very thought sent chills through Olivia. What if the sparks drifted into town? Burned one of their old buildings? Which then sparked the next and the next? Would any of them be safe?

She stared at Joey, who was working beside her, pulling up brush, stacking it in one of the growing piles. Her anxiety was in full bloom. She couldn't let him get hurt. And if the fire made its way into town…

"Mom." Joey tugged at her arm, needing help carrying the brush.

Automatically, she grabbed one side of the pile.

People had been split into different groups. She and Joey were collecting brush and pulling up small tree sprouts.

Residents, mostly ranchers and farmers, brought in their backhoes to dig the trenches. The local construction company had donated all of theirs, as well.

She and Joey were free to help because the clinic was closed. Zeke had decided not to accept patients until they had secured the town and the ranch. So people were still using veterinarians in other towns.

Olivia wasn't entirely displeased by that. Her thoughts were still jumbled since their kiss, and she wasn't certain what the next steps with Zeke would be. Looking over at Joey, she hadn't a clue what she should tell him. Or, based on the distant look in Zeke's eyes the last time she saw him, if there was anything to tell.

"Hey," a familiar voice called from behind her.

Olivia turned, pleased to see Kate and her daughter, Alyssa.

"I never realized we had so much scrub brush out this way," Kate greeted her with a grimace. "I don't even like to weed the garden."

Olivia smiled, relaxing a bit in Kate's company. "Doesn't bother me. But—" she glanced at Alyssa and changed her words, not mentioning her fear of the fire "—it sure isn't fun."

"Alyssa, how about helping Joey with that patch?"

"Sure, Mom."

"She's a sweet girl," Olivia commented.

"The best," Kate agreed. "So, what's bugging you? Besides the obvious." She gestured around their operation.

"Do you think the fire will reach town? Does Tucker know anything?" Olivia guessed the sheriff had the newest information.

"I hope not. The town has survived wildfires in the past,

or so I've been told. Same procedure. Everybody got out here, making sure it was protected. Tuck says this time it's worse. We've never seen the whole state on fire before. And with the drought… But that doesn't mean Rosewood's going to fall to the fire."

Olivia tried to take in what Kate was saying. "I keep thinking I should take Joey and leave."

"And go where?" Kate asked gently. "Austin's surrounded by fires. Same with Houston and San Antonio."

"I just want him to be safe."

"I want Alyssa to stay safe, too. But Rosewood's my home." Kate hesitated. "I understand why you want to run. But at some point you have to take a stand, trust that you're where you should be and know that you're keeping Joey safe in that home. This is where you belong, Olivia."

"You're so sure I belong here?"

"Aren't you?"

This was where Zeke lived, as well as the entire Harrison family, who had welcomed her without reservation, her parents and Kate, the closest friend she had ever made. But did she truly belong?

Kate hugged her shoulders, a quick gesture. "You're on the inside now, Olivia. But I'll stand beside whatever you decide. And if that's to take Joey somewhere else, just promise me that you'll call so that Tuck can make sure the route's safe."

Olivia couldn't speak. She had left so many towns in her life, and once gone it was as though she had never lived in a single one. Always on the outside, yearning to belong.

Kate squeezed her elbow. "Ready to tackle some brush?"

"As ready as I'll ever be," Olivia replied, hope and fear battling for prominence. Again she thought of Zeke, the look in his eyes…and the battle escalated.

* * *

Hours later, exhausted, Joey stretched out on the couch beside his grandmother. She stroked his hair, lifting it away from his still-flushed face.

"We aren't going anywhere," the Colonel announced.

Olivia had given him all the latest updates from Tucker, the real possibility that Rosewood could burn down, everything except her fear. "I don't believe you're thinking this through, Dad."

"Buck up, Olivia. I've never retreated and I don't intend to start now."

"This isn't the army, Dad!" Why had she thought he would listen to reason? She turned toward her mother. "Mom?"

Her mother sighed. "We don't know for certain that the fire will reach Rosewood."

"And if it does?"

"Olivia, where would you have us go?" Mona asked quietly.

"Exactly," the Colonel chimed in. "There are fires in every direction. I'm not stupid. I've been keeping up on the wind and weather tracking. As things stand, the fire may not be able to run a straight course if the predicted storm comes in."

"And if it's a dry storm, it'll just spark more fires," Olivia protested.

"We're *not* evacuating." Olivia knew his decision was final.

"Why don't you and Joey come stay here?" Mona suggested. "We would all feel safer together."

"Thanks, Mom." But the Colonel would shred Olivia's nerves. And if she decided to evacuate, it would be easier to do so from her own house. Plus, she had taken in two of the evacuees. "But we'll stay at home."

Mona's eyes were filled with understanding as she nodded. Olivia wondered if her mother would have chosen to evacuate if on her own. But she had never argued with the Colonel on major issues.

"You'll stay for dinner?" her mother asked, concern flooding her face.

"Of course, Mom. Joey worked hard. I'm sure he's famished."

"And you didn't?" she questioned, knowing her daughter.

"Did what I could."

"Ah." Her mom nodded. "Then you'll be hungry, too."

Olivia appreciated her mother's concern, even her stubborn loyalty to the Colonel, but this made her own decision that much more difficult. If she left, she would be leaving her parents behind.

A few hours later, Olivia pulled into her driveway. Joey stumbled inside the house, immediately heading to his room. Smelling the scent of distant fires growing stronger, she closed his window. He was asleep as soon as he hit the bed. Olivia removed his shoes, then tucked a light cotton blanket over him. Seemed like only yesterday he was a toddler, pleading for extra stories and songs. Swallowing the lump in her throat, she left his room and flipped on the air-conditioning. The door to the guest room was closed, so she hoped her houseguests were getting some rest.

Intending to shut the rest of the windows, she walked into the living room. A quiet knock on the front door startled her.

Her heart skipped a beat. It could be only one person.

Zeke's tall silhouette filled the doorway. She stared up into his face. "Zeke."

"Can I come in?"

"Of course." She opened the door wider and stepped back.

"It's late," he began.

"Not too late," she replied, hope replacing uncertainty.

"I didn't see you today," he said.

"Joey and I were working on the far patch. We were digging up brush and chopping down tiny trees. You said you wouldn't be taking patients, so…" She worried she was babbling, so she stopped talking for a moment, then asked, "Would you like some coffee or iced tea?"

He shook his head.

But Olivia chose to ignore the movement. Instead she walked toward the kitchen. "I think I'll grab something to drink."

She reached the refrigerator, but Zeke was a half step behind, too close for her to open the refrigerator door. Slowly, she turned to face him.

"What are you thinking, Olivia?"

"Nothing." She shrugged one shoulder. "A million things."

"Am I anywhere on that list?"

All over it. "I'm scared, Zeke. I don't want to wait until it's too late to get Joey somewhere safe. And now my parents say they won't evacuate, no matter what."

He studied her eyes, his gaze imprinting her face. Holding her breath, Olivia wondered if he could see past her nervous chatter, past all the doubt, all the wondering.

"Were you going to tell me before you left with Joey?"

Olivia swallowed, wishing she could know how he felt. "Of course," she managed.

"That's something, then." An unfamiliar note of bitterness flavored his words.

"Zeke, it's not a simple decision. I just want to keep Joey safe."

"And you think I can't do that?"

"He's not your responsibility," she protested. "I can't ask you to—"

"You don't have to ask."

She couldn't breathe. There was only a whisper of space between them, yet the tension rose as though they had climbed a tall peak.

Abruptly, Zeke stepped back.

And took the air with him.

"I have to get back to the ranch." His boots thudded as he walked toward the front door.

Trying to get her balance back, she hurried after him. "Zeke?"

He paused.

"You'll be careful, won't you?"

His eyes deepened beyond the night. "Nothing out here that can hurt me." Then he disappeared into the dark as silently as he had arrived.

Olivia gripped the front door, searching. But nothing revealed itself in the shadows. It was then she noticed. Her breathing was ragged, as though she had run and run. Briefly closing her eyes, she wondered if she had. Because she was thinking of running. Even though everything she wanted was right here. In Rosewood.

Chapter Eighteen

The phone rang. Olivia buried her head under the pillow, tugging on the comforter. She had struggled to fall asleep, only managed to do so in the wee hours, her thoughts roiling and battling each other.

The phone continued ringing.

She shot up in bed and grabbed the receiver.

"Olivia, it's Kate."

"Are you all right?"

"I am, but Zeke's not."

Fear made her freeze. "What? No!"

"Olivia! He's not hurt."

"What's wrong, then?"

"The fire's closing in on his ranch. His whole family is helping, but he needs people who know the clinic to help. You know Angie can't. And I thought…"

"Of course! I'll get dressed. Is it safe for Joey?"

"For now."

"Oh, Kate."

"I know. Just go, Olivia."

Grabbing her jeans and a T-shirt, Olivia shouted for Joey.

He emerged from his bedroom, still dressed in the clean

clothes he'd worn to bed. Sleepy, he scratched his head. "What?"

"We have to get out to the ranch."

He awoke with a start. "I have to let Brownie out first."

He insisted on bringing the dog with them, arguing that if the fire did hit the town, Brownie would be trapped.

She'd agreed, urgently needing to hurry, to get to Zeke. Fortunately, her guests slept through the commotion.

The highway was full of every kind of vehicle imaginable. Evacuating families, unsuspecting tourists and ranchers with trailers full of horses and cattle. What normally was a short drive turned into an interminable crawl until they finally reached Zeke's ranch.

Tucker's patrol car was parked on the road, the red lights on top flashing. Pickup trucks with horse trailers were parked haphazardly from the road to the house and beyond.

Remembering how many trailers it had taken to deliver the rescued animals, Olivia knew instantly that there weren't nearly enough to evacuate them all, including Milkdud and Zeke's horses.

When they got close to the clinic, she didn't see Zeke. "Joey, run inside and grab the clipboard with the rescue-animal inventory." Someone had to keep up with whose animals were going where.

Spotting Zeke's brother Ken, she grabbed him. "What's the plan?"

"Chaos," Ken replied with plain, frightening truth. "Mom and Dad, Del and Erica are here. You know Melanie's expecting, so she can't help, and Zeke told her husband to stay home with her in case they have to evacuate. And Heidi's not in town. A lot of neighbors have turned out. And the volunteer fire department is here." He stared around at the dusty acres of confusion. "But…"

"Not nearly enough trailers," she supplied for him. "Has anyone called for backup?"

"I'm not sure. Word's getting around, though."

But not fast enough. Thinking quickly, Olivia rushed back to the office to get phone numbers. Joey was still searching for the clipboard.

"It's over here." Olivia pointed to a wall opposite the one Joey was searching. "We need to call vets in the area. See if they have or know people who have trailers they can bring." She would much rather have Joey inside than anywhere close to the nearing disaster.

"Okay."

Looking around, Olivia wondered where the guests were. Zeke's mom, Nancy, emerged from the living room.

"Oh, good, you're here!" she exclaimed.

"Where else would I be?"

Nancy hugged her. "You stay safe, you hear? It's dangerous out there."

"I'm mostly doing paperwork," Olivia explained, touched by the concern she read in Nancy's eyes. "I am wondering what happened to the people who were staying here."

"Some are helping with the fire. I sent the rest to our house. We have plenty of room."

"You're incredibly generous."

Nancy laughed, shaking her head. "I'm not the only one. I hear you took in a family, as well."

"Only two people," Olivia protested.

Nancy shook her head again. "I'll be connecting water hoses if anyone needs me."

Joey asked Olivia, "Mom?"

"Yes, sweetie." The old affectionate term popped up out of nowhere but her son didn't protest.

"Do you think Zeke's ranch will burn down?"

"What kind of talk is that? I'd better get out there and make sure we know where all the animals are going."

Handing Joey the list, she took the clipboard from him. "You call around to these vets. See if they can send any animal haulers our way."

"What about you, Mom?" A touch of the little boy he had been surfaced in his expression.

"I'll be fine." She held up the clipboard. "Just doing my paperwork outside instead of in here."

Stepping outside, she tipped her face up, wishing she could call on Him for help. But she suspected if she prayed for rain, lightning bolts would appear to join the cacophony of noise that assaulted her ears. Its level had increased in just the time since she had gone into the office. Shading her eyes with one hand, she scanned the area, trying to locate Zeke.

Finally she spotted him on the far perimeter.

She pushed her way through animals and volunteers until she finally caught up to him. "What are you doing?"

He spun around, looking shocked to see her. "What are you doing here?"

"Helping. Where else would I be?" She stared back, wondering at his tone.

He shook his head, still looking baffled, but there was a sliver of something in his expression. Relief? Hope?

She couldn't be sure, but he turned back and surveyed the land again.

"What is it?"

"There aren't enough trailers to move all the animals," Zeke replied, his voice tense.

"I know. Joey's inside calling vets, trying to get more."

"Everyone is using their own trailers or has lent them out. I doubt there's a trailer to be had between here and the coast."

"But if we can't move the animals…" Her voice trailed off.

"That's why I'm considering a last-minute firebreak. It'll mean chopping and digging."

"I know. Will that hold back the fire?"

His expression was grim. "No way to know for sure. But we have to do something."

Blinking, she tried to think of something helpful. "Why don't you talk to the fire chief? See what he thinks?"

"I can't drag him away from town."

"He's already here," she replied excitedly. "Most of the fire department is."

Zeke exhaled, searching the darkening skies. "The fire's getting closer."

She grabbed his arm. "Oh, Zeke! Your home, your clinic."

"Can all be rebuilt. But the animals come first."

"Still…"

"Still, it's wood and stone. What's irreplaceable—" he paused "—is standing right here."

Olivia's heart crumbled as she stood before him, absorbing her love for this man.

"Zeke!" a man hollered.

He didn't move for several moments, then reluctantly looked up. "It's Art, the fire chief."

Still he didn't move.

"Go, Zeke. We have tomorrow. Today we have to make sure the animals do, too."

"My dad said you were a corker."

"Is that good?" she asked, a smile pushing up the corners of her mouth.

"Very good."

The fire chief caught up to them. "Made some calls. Can't find any trailers anywhere."

"I know. I'm thinking we lay a firebreak around the perimeter of the corrals and barn."

"The whole western side," the chief agreed. "If we can stop the fire here, the town has a better chance of escaping it. I'll get the boys together. The wildland fire trucks and firefighters should get here soon."

Olivia held up the clipboard. "I thought I'd make sure we keep a record of where the animals are going."

"Good idea. No telling where the trailers will wind up."

Some of the horses were moved first. People on foot and horseback were rounding up the frightened animals. Drivers backed trailers up near a loading chute, awaiting a turn as other trailers were being filled.

Milkdud mooed pitifully when she was led from her home. Knowing Zeke had nursed her since she was a frail calf, Olivia found herself talking to the cow. "It's okay, Milkdud. Zeke will come get you just as soon as it's safe." She patted the cow's flank. "I'll get the driver's cell-phone number so we can keep up with you."

It didn't take long to fill all the trailers. They were able to get some of the horses and donkeys boarded, as well as the long-term patients from the barn that couldn't be moved. But they were still left with all the sheep, goats and most of the cattle. Olivia hoped Joey was finding some additional trailers.

Suddenly Joey loped toward her. "Mom!"

She met him halfway. "Did you find more trailers?"

"Nope. But everyone said they'd spread the word. Some said they'll call around, but that pretty much everyone had their trailers full."

"Did you call the whole list?"

"I can try the vets farther away," Joey suggested.

"It can't hurt. Just be careful, sweetheart."

For once he didn't give her that "oh, Mom" look. "I will."

Olivia returned to the corral, making sure she had a cell-phone number for every driver. Each agreed to call when they had a final destination.

The acrid smoke bit into the air like a weapon. Olivia's eyes burned. The hot temperature increased as the fire grew closer. Looking up from her clipboard, Olivia clapped one hand across her mouth to silence a scream. Billows of flame-punctured smoke rose above the landscape. If the fire couldn't be stopped, it would not only engulf the ranch, it would head to Rosewood.

What were they going to do?

Searching for Zeke, all she saw were flames. She was near panic when the wildland fire trucks arrived. Firefighters quickly jumped down. Other equipment moved about with grim purpose.

Zeke and Art met with the wildland chief just as the man was ending a radio transmission. Tucker joined them, as well.

"We have a slurry bomber on the way," the wildland chief announced.

"Any new orders?" Art questioned.

"Yep. A suggested evacuation has been issued to Rosewood. I'm not sure if we'll be able to stop this."

"Some people have already pulled out," Tucker said. "Kate's in town helping a few of our elderly people get their things together. Better to evacuate needlessly than wait until it's too late."

So the evacuation wasn't an order. Yet. Olivia looked back at the clinic. It sat as solid as it always had. But the fires to the west proved it wasn't unbreachable. The Colonel's refusal to leave slammed into her thoughts. He wouldn't think of himself as older, possibly in need of help.

Fire didn't respect homes, highways or stubborn people. And then there was Joey.

Should she join the mass exodus on the highway?

Glancing up, she caught Zeke's gaze locked on her. And what about the man she loved? He would never leave the animals that were still on the ranch.

Olivia stood, mesmerized by the fire, the men's voices and noise from the machines washing over her, almost drowned out by the booming roar of the fire itself.

Zeke snagged her arm. She hadn't even seen him walk toward her. "You don't have to stay."

"Neither do you," she pleaded.

His eyes filled with gentle reproach.

"I want to help," she blurted out, refusing to listen to the voice in her head that said, *Run.*

Zeke searched her face, then stroked her cheek. "Yep. A real corker."

Olivia swallowed. "You're not so bad yourself."

Just then the fire emitted a belching boom.

"You don't have to do this, Olivia. You and Joey can go home."

"No, Zeke. You need all the help you can get."

"If you're going to help, you have to wear the right clothes," Zeke replied, his voice gruff.

He nabbed one of the wildland firefighters and helped her get outfitted with Nomex overpants and shirt, which she pulled on over her jeans and T-shirt. Glad she'd worn her boots, she fastened her helmet and pulled on gloves as a shovel was thrust into her hands. Zeke rolled up her pant legs as the firefighter turned up the too-long sleeves.

"Olivia," Zeke began, "if you get too close to the fire, get tired or just plain scared, come back here, understand?"

Olivia met his eyes, his wise, kind eyes. "I can handle it."

Zeke squeezed her arms. "No heroics. I want you safe."

Touched more than she could imagine, her throat dried up, but she managed to smile at him. "Okay."

The firefighter caught her attention. "You ready?"

"Yes."

"Then follow me," he said, carrying a shovel and a pick he called a "Pulaski." Olivia hurried behind him, listening to brief instructions. "Remember, to fire, you're fuel. It's impersonal. We'll be laying line—firebreak—to try to keep it away from here and the town. There'll be some water dropping from the helicopters and slurry from the bomber when it gets here." Stopping, he gazed up at the smoke swirling into the hot blue sky. "Hopefully soon. We'll be working with these folks on the line."

Following their example, Olivia set to work. She recognized several local volunteers like herself in the mix. But everyone was concentrating on their work, and she fell to digging and chopping alongside them. The heat was searing, the noise incredibly deafening, as if a dozen jet engines were running full speed nearby. Soot and ashes drifted over them, sticking to Olivia's sweaty face. Gratefully, she found a kerchief in the back pocket of her Nomex pants and knotted it beneath her helmet like a headband. Time blurred. Had she been here days? Weeks?

In the midst of chopping and digging and raking, she straightened momentarily and watched a couple of the wildland firefighters dash across the widening firebreak to start a backfire on the other side of it.

The safest place in a fire is in the black, she recalled from her brief instructions. A backfire would widen the firebreak even more, creating "black" on the other side, lessening the fuel available to the hungry fire and the chance it might jump the break.

Feeling as if the fire were physically beating her, Olivia

sat down suddenly, her legs refusing to hold her up another minute. This was nothing like clearing brush when the fire was just a faraway concept; this was a blazing monster scorching her with its breath.

In moments "her" firefighter knelt beside her, handing her water to drink. "That's it, you're through. Get outta here."

Olivia wanted to keep working, to make sure Zeke's home was safe. But the fire was stronger than she was. Unable to protest, she rose and headed away from the worst of the heat.

It was a relief to shed the heavy Nomex and leave her equipment behind. She grabbed a bottle of water in a big cooler someone had provided and walked toward the pasture closest to the corral.

Joey and Brownie were right in the middle of the animals, and Olivia called out to her son. "Joey!"

"I'm helping load the animals!" he shouted above the deafening noise.

Olivia looked beyond him, seeing a new trailer being loaded. Heartened that they had gotten some help, she shouted back, "Joey! I need to talk with you."

"In a minute!" he hollered.

Wanting him within her reach, she started toward him when she saw Zeke motion to Joey and point. Her son raced away with Brownie toward the little herd of sheep. Brownie ran around one side and Joey the other, forcing the sheep toward the chute where the trailers waited. *It's as if he's done this all his life.*

She looked back at the fire and decided that although he wouldn't be at her side, he would be farther away from the fire if he worked herding the animals.

Still conflicted, she looked up to see helicopters with

suspended water buckets emptying their contents to douse the flames. Could the water put out the flames? With the massive acres of fire, the giant bucket seemed more like a thimble of water trying to douse a house fire.

Zeke was at the corral literally riding herd on the evacuation. Belatedly, Olivia searched for her clipboard when she saw they were boarding some miniature donkeys. One must be Pansy, her houseguest's pet. She had to collect their information. She couldn't disappoint the little girl.

The clipboard was where she'd left it before donning the Nomex pants and jacket. She retrieved it and nabbed Zeke. "Are you sure Joey's okay?"

Zeke looked out into the pasture. "Let him be, Olivia. Out there helping, he's a wrangler, not just a little boy. He and Brownie really helped with the sheep." Zeke pointed into the pasture, showing her that Joey and the dog were successfully herding a couple of the miniature donkeys their way.

He spared a glance at the fire. In spite of the firebreak, it seemed to know just where to advance to do the most damage. It was like a living thing, coiling, blooming, roaring. And perhaps it did live—it breathed; it consumed; it left waste. Such waste.

Dry junipers exploded as the advancing flames ignited them, sounding like fireworks on steroids. Zeke feared for the animals, his town, his own ranch.

"In they go," he said as the little donkeys entered the trailer. He quickly shut the door.

Despite the arrival of three trailers, there still weren't enough to evacuate all the animals. Joey had done good work calling the area vets, but Zeke had known there wouldn't be many trailers, if any, that hadn't already been committed.

So far the fire hadn't started to circle. If it did, they couldn't lay enough line to protect the northern perimeter. There wasn't enough time or labor. As it was, the firebreak to the west was a stretch. Townspeople kept arriving, most bringing their own spades and picks, a few bringing gas-operated chain saws, as well.

His mother was wetting down his house with an extended hose from the kenneling area. He had tried to dissuade her, worried that she was going to seriously exhaust herself. She'd shooed him off and told him to worry about the animals. And his dad was still wrangling the spooked cattle while on horseback.

Almost all of the adult Harrisons were helping. He prayed silently to protect all the innocent, letting no harm come to any of them.

Zeke turned and spotted Olivia clutching the clipboard like a lifeline. Before she'd turned up, he could have sworn she would be on the highway, fleeing with Joey. When she had appeared, for a moment he was sure he was seeing things.

Now she was covered in soot and ashes, her face smeared and streaked. He'd never seen anything so beautiful.

As he watched, she slipped between the rails of the corral and added the cell number of this newest driver and where he expected to take the load of animals. With Rosewood itself now under a suggested evacuation, it was growing more and more difficult to find a destination. A few people in town had offered to take a few goats each or a horse or cow to put in their backyards until the fire passed.

The town itself had taken all the possible prevention measures. Now they were operating solely on faith that their homes would remain safe.

Zeke gazed in the direction of town, unable to imagine

Rosewood engulfed in fire. It was more than just buildings and roads—it was the caring community, the practice of neighbor helping neighbor, of strangers being welcomed as though they were natives. Swallowing, he silently repeated his prayer.

The flames were marching closer. Ribbons of smoke entwined the pecan trees. Trees that had been there far longer than he'd been alive. He glanced at the familiar sight of his barn, marred by the clouds of dust from hurriedly rounding up the animals. It could all be gone in an instant.

He prayed harder.

Olivia scribbled the last phone number on her clipboard, then turned to see how many animals remained. Far too many.

Where was Joey? she wondered. Ducking to one side, she could see he was again rounding up sheep. As she watched, Brownie raced away across the pasture.

"Brownie!" Joey shouted, rushing after the dog.

"Joey! Joey, come back!" Fear clutched Olivia as her child ran toward the burning woods at the edge of the pasture.

Running as though her life depended on it, she took off, trying to reach Joey.

"Olivia!" Zeke hollered.

"It's Joey!" she screamed. "He's running toward the fire!"

Zeke loped across the pasture, his long legs outdistancing hers in moments. Joey had a good head start and was still out of reach.

But suddenly, without warning, Joey simply disappeared into the fire.

Screaming, she couldn't believe what she was seeing. "No!" The wail emerged from the depth of her soul.

Joey had just disappeared into a wall of smoke. She ran with all her might toward the spot that had swallowed her son.

But strong arms seized her, leaving her arms and legs churning, unwilling to accept that she was not contacting the ground any longer.

"Let me go! My baby's in the fire! Let me *go!*"

"Olivia, stop!"

"No!"

Zeke shook her to get her attention. "I'll go."

"I have to—"

"You have to stay in case I don't make it out. Go get the chief. And pray, Olivia. Pray."

Torn, she saw the determination in his eyes and gave him her ultimate trust. Her child. "All right."

What if he didn't come out, either? She looked toward the sky, invoking the Lord. *Please, keep them safe. Let them both come back to me.*

Ready to crumble, instead she ran toward the nearest group of firefighters. Suddenly people were shouting and moving. One reached the wildland fire chief, who spoke into his radio.

Minutes turned into eternities. Then a new noise filled the air, and she looked up. The big slurry bomber descended and spread a swath of slurry over the burning woods. A large area of fire just short of the pasture went out.

She stood there dumbfounded, and only the sight of Brownie emerging from the smoking ruins of the forest snapped her out of her trance.

In moments Joey followed Brownie, carrying a baby lamb in his arms. "Mom!"

Her chest stuttered as she ran toward him, needing to touch him to make certain he was really alive.

"Zeke?" she asked in a shaky voice. Would the Lord take the man she loved?

Joey put down the lamb and hugged her. Hard.

Oh, no. It couldn't be....

Just then Zeke stumbled from the smoke.

"Zeke covered me until the slime stuff got dumped on us. I think his back is burned."

"Are you okay, sweetheart?"

"Yeah."

Not wanting to leave him, she was glad when the medic arrived with the portable oxygen for him. As soon as he was fitted with oxygen, she tore off toward Zeke.

"You're alive!" she blurted out just as tears gushed from her eyes. Not bothering to wipe them away, she grabbed his arm, never wanting to let go. "You could have been killed."

"But I wasn't." His face was streaked with deep tracks of soot. "The Lord kept us safe."

"He did, didn't He?" she agreed in tearful relief. "I was so afraid to believe. So afraid to trust Him again."

Zeke pulled her close. "He's always with us, Olivia. Watching out for lambs and little boys."

She sobbed into his shoulder, sobs of relief, gratitude and the release of repressed emotions about Ted's death.

And Zeke let her. Until the last ragged breath hiccuped and she sighed.

Zeke pulled off his hat, wiping the sweat from his forehead. "Now, let's go see how our boy's doing."

Our boy? Olivia thought she might start crying all over again. Instead she took Zeke's hand. Then, like a thunderbolt, she remembered. "Your back! Joey said you got burned."

"It's not bad." Zeke shrugged off her concern.

Knowing he wouldn't complain, she pulled him toward the medic, insisting that he get checked out.

"Mostly first degree, some second," the medic pronounced. "And this bit could be third degree. We need to get you both in the ambulance."

"Olivia, go with Joey."

"What about you?"

Zeke looked at the medic. "You can bandage this, right?"

Reluctantly, the medic nodded. "You still need to go to the hospital."

"After the fire's out or we get all the animals evacuated."

"Zeke," Olivia pleaded again.

Again gentle reproach filled his eyes.

And Olivia knew he wouldn't budge.

Chapter Nineteen

Joey checked out fine at the hospital. Some smoke inhalation, but Zeke had protected him well, taking the brunt of the smoke and flames. When Olivia asked if Joey could go back into the smoky air, the doctor reminded her that all the air in the area was tinged with smoke.

The road back to the ranch was a nightmare. More than half of Rosewood had turned out to help fight the fire despite the threat to their own homes.

Reaching Kate by phone, Olivia learned that the elderly had been evacuated. And some families with small children had chosen to leave. But most had decided to fight for their homes, their town. Most had wet their houses and yards, the buildings on Main Street. But when they heard about the fire threatening Zeke's ranch and the rescue animals, many had chosen to help.

If what the wildland chief had predicted was true, the large firebreak would help the town, as well.

Olivia gazed at her son, still filled with gratitude that he had survived. "Joey, what possessed you to run into the fire?"

"Did you see how Brownie kept running around and around me? When he took off across the pasture, I could tell he wanted me to follow him. Mom, he knew that baby lamb was out there, that it had gotten lost from its mother when we were trying to herd them toward the corral." He punctuated his story with hand motions, his eyes alive and bright. "Brownie went right to the lamb, and I grabbed it up, but by then the fire cut us off."

He took a swallow of his soda, then continued, "When we started herding the animals to the trailers, it looked like the fire might get us, so the fire chief told us that if the fire started burning too close and we couldn't outrun it, to run into the black."

"Run into the black," Olivia echoed. "That's what my firefighter told me when I went to help on the firebreak."

"Yeah! So that's what I did when we got to the lamb. Couldn't go back to the pasture, so we ran into the black. It was still hot, but not as hot as the fire. Then the fire roared up past this huge tree. Then Zeke was there. He was like Superman, Mom. There wasn't any way out. The fire was all around us, but Zeke didn't panic, just dug a hole in the dirt so I could lay my head in it. Then he covered me up. I thought we might get burned to death...."

Olivia fought the emotions threatening to overwhelm her.

"But Zeke told me to pray. I asked him why God let stuff like Dad dying and fires to happen. He said he didn't know but that we have to always believe. So I prayed with him. Then all the slimy stuff fell on us and the fire, and we got out. It worked, Mom."

A single tear slipped down her cheek. Yes, it had worked. All three of them had prayed. And the Lord had answered. *Believe,* Zeke had said. Olivia felt something new inside, a feeling other than gratitude and relief. She thought it might be her renewed faith.

Finally reaching the ranch, they stared at the blackened

woods. Flames still leaped beyond the extinguished area, but helicopters with water buckets bombarded the fire from the air as firefighters fought it on the ground.

Where was Zeke?

"Mom, can Brownie and I go back and help?"

"Not on the fire line. You can make some more calls. There's a list of all the sanctuaries in my desk."

He and Brownie started to leave.

"And don't go rescueing any more lambs, okay?"

He smiled. "Okay."

Olivia started searching for Zeke. She walked the corral, rounded the pasture, then went to the firebreak area. The heat was still intense. But the backfire seemed to be holding. And the slurry had doused more flames while she had been gone.

But still no Zeke.

Stomach knotted, she walked back. As she passed the barn, she peeked inside. Zeke sat on a hay bale. A medic was changing the bandage on his back.

She started to greet him when the medic peeled the old bandage off. She was appalled to see the deep, blistering burns on his back.

"Zeke!"

He turned at her voice. "It's not as bad as it looks."

"And how would you know how it looks? The burns are on your back! Zeke, you need to go to the hospital and get that treated."

"Listen to the lady," the medic interjected.

"Not just yet." Zeke reached for her hands. "There are no more trailers to be had. I have to stay."

She wanted to shake him, tell him he had sacrificed enough, that she didn't want him in danger. "But—"

"The wildland chief says that if we can stop the fire here, Rosewood will be safe."

"I know how important the town is to you."

"And to you, I hope."

A town important to her? The thought was strange. Then she remembered the welcome she had received, the friendships she had formed. The town *was* important to her. Rosewood had become more than a stopover. It was home. It was where she belonged.

By nightfall they declared the fire 70 percent contained. The wildland chief and the volunteer fire department's chief were in agreement. The path to Rosewood had been stopped. And the suggested evacuation had been rescinded.

Smoke overwhelmed the air, filling their lungs. In the far distance, they could still see fire licking its way south. South of Rosewood. South of Zeke's ranch.

The remaining animals hadn't yet settled down, some still pawing the ground. A few goats butted the rails of the corrals. But they were all alive.

Joey had bathed the lamb he had rescued. The little guy had been covered in the slurry that had saved their lives. Now he was back with his mother.

"No more delays," Olivia told Zeke. "Time to get you checked out at the hospital."

Some of Zeke's exhaustion showed in his eyes. "You don't ever give up, do you?"

"Not when I have something worth fighting for."

Disregarding his wounds, he pulled her close. "That right?"

She started to nod. But Zeke cupped the back of her neck, his lips touching hers.

The remainder of Olivia's resistance tumbled. She loved him as she'd never thought she could. Every bit of him.

* * *

When he pulled back, she reached up to caress his jaw, to rest her fingers on his lips.

Zeke lightly kissed those same fingers, wondering how he had come to be so blessed, how this incredible woman was now his.

He kissed her again, wanting to be sure this wasn't a dream.

Scattered applause and loud whoops erupted.

Startled, they both turned to see Zeke's parents, two brothers and his sister Erica all smiling and clapping.

"About time!" Erica declared.

Ken and Del cheered their agreement.

Flushing, Olivia looked up at Zeke.

Seeing the clear depth of her feelings reflected in her eyes, he grinned. "Well, don't just stand there gawking. Come congratulate my fiancée." He looked back at Olivia. "If she'll have me."

Lips trembling, Olivia held tight to his hand. "Forever?"

He reached for her, tugging her close to him again. "No running away. No more new places. We're right where we belong."

When they finally got Zeke to the hospital, his burns turned out to be fairly serious. The third-degree burns were confined to the middle of his back, but second- and first-degree burns encircled the deepest ones. The doctor wanted to keep him overnight for observation, but Zeke refused.

"All I want to do is go home. Have to see with my own eyes that the house is still standing."

"You saw it before we left," Olivia protested. "If the doctor thinks you should stay—"

"He said my lungs are fine." He pointed to the cannula that was pumping oxygen into him.

"He *said* you had a lot of smoke inhalation," Olivia corrected. "And your poor back…"

"I wouldn't have it any other way. If something had happened to Joey…" His deep voice cracked. It was just a small shift, but Olivia was so in tune with him, she knew. Squeezing his hand, she gave in to the tears that had been bottled up since she had seen his wounds.

"What's this?" Zeke sat up in the bed.

She shook her head, despite the tears that ran down her cheeks. "If you hadn't run after Joey…"

"The Lord was with me, Olivia. There's no other explanation. He's with you now, isn't He?"

She nodded her head as she fought her tears.

Zeke squeezed her hand. "That's forever, too."

Forever? She, the one who had never belonged anywhere. Now she had a town, faith, friends and a man she loved beyond tomorrow.

Blessings. It was a small word for all that she had been given. Meeting Zeke's eyes, she knew they had just begun.

Chapter Twenty

Olivia had always wanted friends and lots of close family. She just hadn't expected family Harrison-style.

Her head spun with all the help and suggestions thrown her way for the wedding preparations.

She knew in an instant who she wanted as her matron of honor. Kate. Kate, who was forever bringing her a copy of every bridal magazine.

Olivia hadn't expected everyone else to be as swept up in the preparations as herself. Zeke waved his hands and backed away anytime the wedding chatter started.

Sitting at one of the tables in the Tea Cart, Olivia could barely find her cup of tea among the outspread pages. "Kate, I don't really think I need all this."

"They're just a jumping-off point." She flipped a few pages and pointed to an elegant dress with a long, flowing train.

Olivia's eyes widened. "Kate, this is my second wedding. It just wouldn't be appropriate."

"It's Zeke's first," Kate reminded her gently. "And I was about to say I like the lines of the dress without the train. It has a beautiful neckline and look how the sleeves are fretted."

"It is beautiful," Kate admitted. "But to get it as simple as I want, I'd have to get it custom-made. No one's going to have a simple dress that would suit me."

Kate smiled, then wiggled her eyebrows. "Now, aren't you lucky to be living in Rosewood? Our costume shop also designs wedding gowns. Emma McAllister has made the most beautiful gowns I've ever seen. No two are alike and they truly fit the bride's personality. She sold the shop to her assistant, but she still helps out when there's a special wedding gown to design."

"Do you think she…? Oh, she doesn't even know me." Olivia shook her head.

"Would I have mentioned her if I thought she wouldn't be interested? We three have something in common. We're not Rosewood natives, but the town has adopted us as though we were. What do you say? Are you game?"

The stars in Olivia's eyes, which hadn't dimmed since Zeke proposed, now sparkled. "I think I am."

"Son, usually you have someone your own age as the best man," Robert protested. "What about one of your brothers?"

Zeke laughed. "It's the tux, isn't it?" His father was known to live in jeans except when attending church. And the tie and suit came off as soon as he returned home.

"Ken and Del might feel left out," Robert argued. "And they've been your best buddies for years."

"Not the best, Dad. That's always been you."

It took a few moments for Robert to speak. "Thank you, son. You don't know what that means to me."

Zeke knew. He would still be half a man without his father's wisdom and guidance. He patted his father's shoulder. "I'll draft Ken and Del as ushers. We'll need them just to seat our herd."

His father laughed. Then he met Zeke's gaze. "You found the right one."

Knowing his father was talking about Olivia, Zeke smiled. "I know."

Robert's eyes softened. "You're thinking I like happy endings."

"No, Dad. I'm thinking *I* like happy endings."

Kate was right. Emma McAllister was a magician. She had sewn silk and lace together to create a dress beyond her dreams. Soft ivory silk was draped in a subtle empire style, while vintage lace at the throat drew the eye upward. The incredible fretted sleeves, a throwback to the gorgeous gowns of the 1940s, came to a point on each hand. Tiny pearls edged the heirloom lace.

Larger pearls had been woven into the simple headpiece. Her hair was swept up and held in place seemingly by random pearls. A creation of Emma's, also gorgeous.

Olivia lifted her left hand in the sunlight, the diamond ring twinkling as she remembered.

"I have something for you," Zeke began.

"You already gave me your heart. I don't need anything else."

His eyes took on that deep color that only emotion could evoke. And he kissed her gently.

Again the very air whispered the love flowing between them.

Leaning back, Zeke knelt and took her hand.

Olivia gasped.

"You deserve a proper proposal. Olivia, I love you. I think I have since the day I met you over a boxful of baby chicks. And it's only grown since then. Olivia, will you marry me?"

Trembling, her face crinkled as she tried to stop the tears of joy. "Yes," she warbled.

Zeke pulled a jeweler's box from his jacket pocket. Taking her hand again, he slid on a perfect emerald-cut diamond engagement ring.

"I love you," she breathed. Then she watched the ring sparkle in the afternoon sunlight. "It's beautiful."

Zeke stood up. "Then it matches you."

Kate fussed with the hem of Olivia's gown, bringing her back to the present. "Emma outdid herself. This is the most beautiful dress ever. You look like a princess."

"I feel like a princess," Olivia confessed. She smoothed her hands over the silken sides of the dress. "This is something out of a dream."

"Even better since it's real," Kate replied, her hands resting on her tummy.

Despite everything going on, Olivia narrowed her eyes. Was that a little mound forming? "Kate?"

Her friend followed Olivia's gaze, then nodded.

"Oh, Kate!" Olivia threw her arms around her, hugging her. "I'm so happy for you."

"Me, too," Kate admitted, her face nearly crumpling into tears of joy. "I almost can't believe it."

"Why didn't you say something?"

"I didn't want to take anything away from your special day."

"Take away?" Olivia questioned. "It's the best present I could imagine! Now I *know* prayers are answered."

"You mean…?"

"Yes, I've been praying for you. Kate, you're the best friend I've ever had, and this will be the happiest baby in the world!"

Kate's hormones kicked in and she started to cry. Then Olivia felt the threat of tears, as well.

"Oh, no!" Kate dabbed at her eyes. "Don't you dare cry! It'll ruin your makeup!"

Olivia sniffed. "It would be worth it."

"No. You look perfect and you're going to stay that way. What kind of matron of honor would I be to let your mascara run?" Kate laughed as the last of her tears evaporated. Cocking her head, she listened to the organ music. "It's time. Ready?"

Truly, for the first time in her life, Olivia was. "Yes."

Kate collected Olivia's bouquet of ivory roses. "Then I guess we're on."

Olivia settled the fragrant bouquet in her hands, her pulse quickening as she thought of Zeke waiting for her.

Kate picked up her own small bouquet, a solitary calla lily that complemented her light green dress. A color that had been chosen to match her pretty green eyes.

Leaving the bridal room, they walked out to the church foyer, where the Colonel and Joey waited. Olivia didn't care that it wasn't traditional. Both of them were giving her away. Joey had taken the news of their marriage plans with excitement. He idolized Zeke, and after their experience in the fire, they had bonded deeply.

And despite not being able to please her father, Olivia loved him. For all his gruffness, he had a good heart.

"Well, men," Olivia greeted them. "Do I look okay?"

Joey grinned. "Yeah."

"You look beautiful, Livvy." It was a nickname he hadn't used since she was a child.

Impulsively, she hugged him. "Thanks, Dad."

The organ's song came to an end.

Then the wedding march began.

With her arms hooked through theirs, the trio walked up the aisle to the trumpeting music.

Unable to focus on anything but Zeke looking incredibly handsome in his tuxedo, she didn't notice that all the pews were full.

Sunlight filtered through the stained-glass windows, sending rainbows of muted light over the sanctuary. Everywhere the sunbeams touched, they warmed the space.

As she and Zeke stood on the altar, she listened to the age-old wedding vows, repeated their promises.

"I now pronounce you husband and wife," the minister declared.

Zeke claimed her lips.

Then they turned to face friends and family. It seemed that all of Rosewood had turned out. Barely making it to the foyer, they were mobbed. People Olivia didn't know shook her hand; some kissed her cheek. Seeing her mother, Olivia broke into a smile when she saw how happy she looked. Reaching out a hand, Olivia made certain she and the Colonel weren't pushed out by all the Harrisons.

"Pictures," the photographer told her.

Those could wait. She would never forget these moments.

In another nontraditional move, they had decided to host the reception at the ranch.

Many hugs later, she and Zeke drove to the ranch in his well-decorated Suburban.

The town café and the bakery were providing the catering. The Harrison siblings had decorated the ranch the previous night.

As they approached the ranch, it looked beautiful.

"Pinch me," Olivia said.

Zeke laughed. "I'd rather kiss you."

She leaned over to kiss his cheek.

He glanced in the rearview mirror. "That'll have to do for now." He turned in the driveway and stopped the truck.

"What?" she asked.

He pointed to the clinic sign engraved with *HVC*. Beneath the letters was a new engraving: Zeke & Olivia Harrison.

"You belong," he asserted. "Says so right there."

"And you," she replied, knowing his past.

They kissed again.

Car and truck horns behind them began honking.

Reluctantly, they pulled apart.

Zeke drove to the ranch house.

"Everything looks wonderful!" Olivia exclaimed as Zeke helped her out of the vehicle. "Your family is amazing."

"*Our* family," he corrected, taking her arm, tucking her close to him.

Zeke glanced down at her violet eyes. She was so beautiful, inside and out. The vulnerability that used to lurk in her eyes was gone. Instead they sparkled. It was as though she was whole again.

People soon filled the house and yard. A very pregnant Angie and her husband waved. Kate and Tucker glowed, looking like newlyweds themselves. Harrisons were everywhere. Olivia was pleased to see that Nancy had pulled Mona aside and the two were laughing and talking together. Robert and the Colonel were talking, as well.

Zeke slipped an arm around her waist. "Mrs. Harrison?"

Olivia turned into his embrace. "Yes, Mr. Harrison?"

His gaze was long, intense. "You really are Mrs. Harrison."

She nodded.

"Forever?"

Olivia was right where she belonged, in the arms of the

man she loved, in the town that welcomed her without reserve. At last. She wasn't out of step any longer.

Her heart was overcome with love. Yes, it was forever.
Even that wouldn't be long enough for her to show Zeke
how much she loved him.

As she lifted her face for his kiss, the word simmered
in the air, lilted with the breeze. "Forever."

* * * * *

Dear Reader,

The year of the great Texas fires was 2011. Millions of trees were destroyed and countless animals either perished or were displaced.

Fires consumed the entire state, scorching land from the Panhandle to the Gulf Coast. But the spirit of the people never flagged. Strangers offered land and feed for animals. Other strangers opened their homes to people who had evacuated or been burned out of their homes.

The enduring courage of giving from neighbor to neighbor and stranger to stranger stands testament to the people of Texas. It's often said Texans brag of all that's biggest in their state. They've shown it is their hearts and giving spirit that stand so tall.

In a time when we're not all certain where we belong, it's in these open hearts that we find welcome. I hope you, too, will find a sense of belonging on this journey to Rosewood. And, perhaps, fall in love once again.

God bless,

Bonnie K. Winn

Questions for Discussion

1. Once widowed, do you think Olivia should have given in to her parents' wishes to move in with them? To send Joey to military school? Why or why not?

2. Zeke felt the need to push away a serious relationship. Did you understand his reasons for doing so?

3. Many foster homes, like the Harrisons', provide a wonderful upbringing for children. Others are not as kind. Faced with placing a child in the care system, what would you do?

4. Do you feel Joey's acting out was the result of losing his father? Could Olivia have done anything differently to change the outcome?

5. The town of Rosewood, Texas, has such a strong sense of community. If the town had truly suffered in the fire, how do you think they would have reacted?

6. Did you understand Olivia's feeling of never belonging? Of feeling she was just out of step with everyone else? Have you ever felt this way yourself? Discuss.

7. Belonging is the universal theme of the book. Did that resonate with you?

8. Have you ever been part of a blended family? How did that affect your life? Your family? Discuss.

9. Olivia lost her husband in a violent manner. We often think crime is something that happens only to

other people. Has a crime changed or touched your life in any way?

10. Can you envision the happy family Zeke, Olivia and Joey are destined to be? Do you think they have found that forever family?

LICNM0714

REQUEST YOUR FREE BOOKS!

2 FREE INSPIRATIONAL NOVELS
PLUS 2
FREE
MYSTERY GIFTS

Love Inspired

YES! Please send me 2 FREE Love Inspired® novels and my 2 FREE mystery gifts (gifts are worth about $10). After receiving them, if I don't wish to receive any more books, I can return the shipping statement marked "cancel." If I don't cancel, I will receive 6 brand-new novels every month and be billed just $4.74 per book in the U.S. or $5.24 per book in Canada. That's a saving of at least 21% off the cover price. It's quite a bargain! Shipping and handling is just 50¢ per book in the U.S. and 75¢ per book in Canada.* I understand that accepting the 2 free books and gifts places me under no obligation to buy anything. I can always return a shipment and cancel at any time. Even if I never buy another book, the two free books and gifts are mine to keep forever.

105/305 IDN F47Y

Name	(PLEASE PRINT)	

Address		Apt. #

City	State/Prov.	Zip/Postal Code

Signature (if under 18, a parent or guardian must sign)

Mail to the **Harlequin® Reader Service:**
IN U.S.A.: P.O. Box 1867, Buffalo, NY 14240-1867
IN CANADA: P.O. Box 609, Fort Erie, Ontario L2A 5X3

Are you a subscriber to Love Inspired books
and want to receive the larger-print edition?
Call 1-800-873-8635 or visit www.ReaderService.com.

* Terms and prices subject to change without notice. Prices do not include applicable taxes. Sales tax applicable in N.Y. Canadian residents will be charged applicable taxes. Offer not valid in Quebec. This offer is limited to one order per household. Not valid for current subscribers to Love Inspired books. All orders subject to credit approval. Credit or debit balances in a customer's account(s) may be offset by any other outstanding balance owed by or to the customer. Please allow 4 to 6 weeks for delivery. Offer available while quantities last.

Your Privacy—The Harlequin® Reader Service is committed to protecting your privacy. Our Privacy Policy is available online at www.ReaderService.com or upon request from the Harlequin Reader Service.

We make a portion of our mailing list available to reputable third parties that offer products we believe may interest you. If you prefer that we not exchange your name with third parties, or if you wish to clarify or modify your communication preferences, please visit us at www.ReaderService.com/consumerchoice or write to us at Harlequin Reader Service Preference Service, P.O. Box 9062, Buffalo, NY 14269. Include your complete name and address.

LI13R